THE SQUADRON'S UMBRELLA

THE SQUADRON'S UMBRELLA

ALPHONSE ALLAIS

Translated and with an introduction, notes,
& illustrations by Doug Skinner

2015

THE SQUADRON'S UMBRELLA

by Alphonse Allais

Translated from the French by Doug Skinner

ISBN-13 978-0-692-39212-6

FIRST AMERICAN EDITION
March, 2015

Cover and book design by Norman Conquest

ACKNOWLEDGEMENTS:

This collection was originally published in France in 1893 under the title *Le parapluie de l'escouade*.

Facing page: contemporary silhouette of Allais

BLACK SCAT BOOKS
Sublime Art & Literature
BlackScatBooks.com

CONTENTS

OPENING THE UMBRELLA

lphonse Allais was born October 26, 1854, in the northern town of Honfleur. His father was a pharmacist, and the family expected Alphonse to follow the family trade. At eighteen, he was packed off to Paris to study at the School of Pharmacy; he also filled prescriptions in a couple of Parisian shops.

Paris had attractions far more seductive than chemistry class, however, and young Alphonse preferred sipping absinthe in cafes, seeing shows in theaters and cabarets, dating dancers, and generally whooping it up. He started contributing to periodicals, mostly jokes and one-liners at first. In papers like *Le Tintamarre*, he invented or popularized such forms as the fable-express (a short fable ending in a pun) and the autograph (a joke ending with a pun on someone's name). He became particularly known for his *combles* (acmes):

The acme of caution: To walk on your hands, so tiles won't fall on your head.

The acme of thrift: When in the park, to gather grass for your rabbits.

The acme of skill: To learn to tell time with a barometer.

The acme of affectation: To stay at home, and play the piano every hour and half hour, so your neighbors think you have a musical clock.

The acme of courtesy: To put fallen leaves back on the tree.

In 1881, Rodolphe Salis opened Le Chat Noir on the Boulevard Rochechouart. Conceived to evoke the age of Louis XIII, its waiters wore splendid livery, and Salis proudly displayed the skull of Louis XIII as a child. The doorman was told to admit only painters and poets, and to refuse the military and clergy. It was one of the first cabarets, and presented programs of poets, singers, and monologists; its shadow puppet plays, designed by some of the liveliest young artists in Paris, were a sensation.

Allais became a regular, and was soon beating a drum for the shadow plays, reciting an occasional monologue, and playing practical jokes on guests and regulars.

The next year, Salis started a weekly paper, also called *Le Chat Noir*. Allais wrote for it from the beginning, and eventually became its editor. By this time, the career in pharmacy had quietly evaporated.

His contributions to *Le Chat Noir* became more ambitious than his earlier squibs. He still wrote humorous pieces, but also short stories, often in a Romantic or gothic vein, and articles promoting the cabaret and plugging books by its regulars. He amused himself and his readers with his prolonged ridicule of one of Paris's leading theater critics, Francisque Sarcey.[1] He mercilessly parodied Sarcey's rambling style, and published rave reviews of the cabaret's shows under his byline.

In 1892, a new daily paper, *Le Journal*, was launched by an interesting character named Fernand Xau. A former manager of the Buffalo Bill Wild West Show, of all things, he had established himself as a journalist with a home interview with Émile Zola. He started the paper as "a literary journal for a sou," aimed at workers, teachers, and shopkeepers. It leaned to the left, and attracted fine writers, including Zola, Octave Mirbeau, and Georges Courteline.

Allais started contributing with the second issue. He had a regular column, *La vie drôle* ("The Funny Life"). At first, he kept writing for *Le Chat Noir*, but had to give it up in 1893. The cabaret's paper itself folded in 1897, with the death of Salis.

Allais's work changed when he started working for *Le Journal*. He didn't have room for longer narratives ("my space is strictly limited," he often complained to readers), and took to writing shorter and more topical pieces. He was also catering to a more general audience than the Bohemians of Montmartre; he sometimes lamented that he was reduced to entertaining traveling salesmen. With deadlines looming twice a week, he became expert at padding (as the French put it, *tirer à la ligne*), and at spinning out amusing copy when he had nothing to say. His elegance, scientific curiosity, preoccupation with language and logic, and flashes of cruelty inspired Alfred Jarry (particularly in his columns for *La Revue Blanche* and *Le Canard Sauvage*), as well as succeeding generations of Surrealists, Pataphysicians, and Oulipians.

---

1 See *How I Became an Idiot* by Francisque Sarcey [Alphonse Allais] Black Scat Classic Interim Edition #00 (2012); translated from the French by Doug Skinner

He published his first collection, *À se tordre* (*Double Over*) in 1891. It was followed by *Vive la Vie!* in 1892 and *Pas de Bile!* in 1893. With his fourth collection, *Le parapluie de l'escouade* (*The Squadron's Umbrella*), also from 1893, he set exclamation points aside, and turned to army slang: new recruits were sent to fetch the squadron's umbrella, as American soldiers were once sent after a left-handed monkey wrench.

It's not quite clear how Allais chose the material for his quasi-annual compilations. More than one reader has puzzled over the fact that some of the columns he picked were weaker than the ones he excluded. I can understand regretting the gems, but I find his selections cogent and savvy mixtures of different styles and approaches.

The Squadron's Umbrella contains many of Allais's columns from *Le Journal*, from late 1892 and early 1893. (I've tracked down the original publication dates; they're listed in the notes, for the curious). They include interviews with a kangaroo and with the President of France, anecdotes from his student years, and commentaries on news stories of the day. Several pieces from *Le Chat Noir* are also included, going back to 1886; they tend to be more like short stories than newspaper columns. "The False Blasphemer" and "Posthumous," both from 1886, are samples of Allais's earlier style. And he leads off the collection with a classic display of narrative logic, "Like the Others."

The characters in the stories present some problems for the translator. They're usually either real people, familiar to the original readers but often obscure today, or fictional creatures with puns for names.

For the latter, after some hemming and hawing, I've decided not to substitute English equivalents, unless they're just passing jokes. In the first story, for example, Madeleine Bastye remains as her creator christened her, and I explain in the notes that she was named after a Parisian bus line. That seemed better than turning to the transit system of London or New York. As Allais himself admitted, the joke names really weren't that funny, but they did become part of his style.

For the former, I will have to refer you to the notes. Allais invokes journalists, politicians, actors, scientists, cyclists, poets, doctors, playwrights, and occultists of the time. Several of his colleagues from Le Chat Noir show up, including his fellow Honfleurais, Erik

Satie. Albert Caperon, better known as Captain Cap,[2] the hero of many later stories, makes his first appearance. Francisque Sarcey, too, waddles onstage again, although Allais was no longer permitted to swipe his byline.

Allais also included two translations from the American press: a brief piece by Mark Twain and a report of a medical anomaly. He was unaware, however, that the first was not actually by Twain, and that the second was later revealed as a hoax. It may seem quixotic to translate them back into English, but Allais did rework them in his versions.

So, open the umbrella, and enjoy the downpour. The consummate preface elucidates the title's relation to the contents, presaging similar non sequiturs by Boris Vian (*Autumn in Peking*)[3] and Robert Benchley (*20,000 Leagues Under the Sea, or David Copperfield*). As usual, the reader should be wary: a popular song about an umbrella is indeed mentioned in "The False Blasphemer."

Doug Skinner
New York City
February, 2015

---

2 *Captain Cap: His Adventures, His Ideas, His Drinks* by Alphonse Allais. Translated by Doug Skinner. Black Scat Books (2013)

3 *Autumn in Peking* by Boris Vian. Translated by Paul Knobloch. Tam Tam Books (2005)

PREFACE

I have entitled this book *The Squadron's Umbrella* for two reasons, which I ask the reader's indulgence to tick off before him.

1. There is no mention, in my volume, of umbrellas of any kind.

2. The vital question of the squadron, considered as a unit of combat, is not even broached.

Under such conditions, any hesitation would be an act of sheer madness; I did not, therefore, waver for a second.

I hope that this candid explanation will win me the esteem of the masses, and that these last will purchase, by the carload, *The Squadron's Umbrella,* both for their own enjoyment, and to send to their friends in the Republic of Argentina.

THE AUTHOR

LIKE THE OTHERS

Little Madeleine Bastye would have been the most exquisite woman of the century, without her deplorable habit of being unfaithful to her lovers: sometimes at the drop of a hat, sometimes even without a hat.

At the time that our story begins, her lover was an excellent lad named Jean Passe (of the firm Jean Passe et Desmeilleurs).

An honest soul, this Jean Passe, and, we hasten to add, a shining example of Parisian commerce.

And besides, he loved his little Madeleine so!

The first time that Madeleine cheated on Jean, Jean said to Madeleine:

"Why did you cheat on me with that man?"

"Because he is handsome!" Madeleine replied.

"Fine!" grumbled Jean.

Omnipotence of love! Irresistibility of will! When Jean returned that evening, he was transfigured, and so handsome that the Holy Archangel Michael, next to him, would have seemed as ugly as sin itself.

The second time that Madeleine cheated on Jean, Jean said:

"Why did you cheat on me with that man?"

"Because he is rich!" Madeleine replied.

"Fine!" grumbled Jean.

And the next day, Jean invented a process permitting, with a minimum of labor, the transformation of horse dung into mauve velour.

The Americans fought for the patent with dollars, and even with eagles (the eagle is a gold coin worth 20 dollars. At the present time, the eagle represents exactly 104 francs and 30 centimes of our money).

The third time that Madeleine cheated on Jean, Jean said:

"Why did you cheat on me with that man?"

"Because he is funny!" Madeleine replied.

"Fine!" grumbled Jean.

And he headed for the Ollendorff bookstore, where he bought *Double Over*, the exquisite volume by our charming colleague Alphonse Allais.

He read and reread this truly unique work, and absorbed it so thoroughly, and so well, that Madeleine almost died of laughter that night.

The fourth time that Madeleine cheated on Jean, Jean said:

"Why did you cheat on me with that man?"

"Ah, well!" Madeleine replied.

And a curious glint came into Madeleine's little eyes. Jean understood, and grumbled, "Fine!"

.....

I deeply regret that this is not a pornographic story, for I suspect that the reader would not be bored with the account of what Jean did.

.....

The fifth time that Madeleine cheated on Jean...

Oh, bother!

The eleven hundred fortieth time that Madeleine cheated on Jean, Jean said to Madeleine:

"Why did you cheat on me with that man?"

"Because he is an assassin!" Madeleine replied.

"Fine!" grumbled Jean.

And Jean killed Madeleine.

It was approximately around this time that Madeleine lost the habit of cheating on Jean.

THE SOCIAL QUESTION

I was somewhat surprised — shall I admit it? — to receive, yesterday evening, a word from President Carnot, inviting me to the Elysée as soon as possible. "Urgent," added the note.

My relations with M. Carnot, quite cordial at the beginning of his political career, had cooled considerably afterwards; at first, after that regrettable scene at the Moulin Rouge that is still so fresh in all of our minds, then because of M. Carnot's strange obstinacy in excluding me from any nonpartisan cabinet. (I explained myself on this question, here, some two months ago.)

Nevertheless, I did not hesitate to answer his call. Perhaps the security of the state was at stake.

M. Carnot rushed over at once, and warmly grasped my hands, calling me his dear Alphonse. Then he asked what I would *have*.

"A glass of sugar water, with a bit of orange blossom," was my response.

(I never drink anything else, and am the better for it.)

"But that's not all," the head of state continued briskly. "I didn't invite you here for no reason. We're quite bothered, just now, with the social question. I know your almost legendary ingenuity; do you have a solution for the social question?"

"My child," I answered with a gentle smile, "do I not have a solution for everything?"

"I drink your words."

"Let me, my dear Sadi, compare society to a ladder."

Mild astonishment passed over the features of the grandson of the organizer of the victory.

"A ladder," I continued, "is usually composed of two uprights, and a number of rungs or steps, varying with the length of the device.

"The parallel rungs are set perpendicularly into the inner faces of the uprights. But surely you know all this as well as I, you the pride of the Polytechnic?"

M. Carnot bowed.

"When a certain number of people are called (or, is called) to scale the ladder, it is preferable that they disperse themselves upon all of the rungs, instead of crowding onto just one."

"Of course."

"Yes, but here's the problem: those who are confined to the inferior rungs (as I call the lower ones), subject to social humidity, jostled by the pustular toads of ill fortune, malarial victims of a filthy society, envy those on high, who lounge upon rungs of velvet and gold, up there in the clear azure of the heavens..."

And, since I was getting carried away, like a drunken poet, M. Carnot brought me back to the question.

"Well," I concluded, "here's the solution: It is monstrous that some of our citizens are fatally condemned, forever, to a patrimony of distress, misery, and hard work (the worst of evils), while other young sports need only be born to lead an existence of idleness, kept women, and aluminum bicycles. The true motto of society should be: *Everyone his turn.* Or even better: *The same ones should not always get the gravy train.*"

"Indeed!" muttered the principal tenant of Faubourg-Saint-Honoré.

"If I were you, I would organize an enormous social lottery, with prizes ranging from an income of five hundred thousand pounds to *bugger all* and *zilch*,[1] passing through a thousand intermediary positions. As many prizes as there are French citizens. A drawing every year (on April 1, for a laugh). After that, life would become exquisite and endurable. The tumult of passions would fade away. Envy would fold its hateful green wings. And hope would be reborn! He who held, for the moment, the *bugger all* and *zilch*, would think himself the luckiest of men, in the hope that, in a year, it would be his turn for a little spin around the lake, or, at least, for a nice little income of a thousand pounds."

Visibly astounded at the horizon that I had opened, the President scratched his head. Then, without letting me finish, he added, in an uncanny imitation of Dupuis:

"That's it, the solution to the social question! That's it!"

---

1. Vulgar expression corresponding roughly to what mathematicians call *zero*.

TRIPOLI

To Hermann Paul.

There was a man in my company whose name was Lapouille, but whom we baptized the *Man*, because of an incident that had occurred to him.

As a sort of parenthesis, here is the incident:

Confined to the barracks — which happened more than was his fair share — our excellent Lapouille decided, nevertheless, to take a salutary little stroll in town, which continued until eleven in the evening.

So that, upon his return to camp, he was invited by the master sergeant to conclude in the guardhouse the evening which had started so promisingly.

Lapouille, without a murmur, donned the customary uniform, shouldered his pallet, and headed, with a philosophical tread, to the brig.

"What, another?" cried the sergeant of the guard. "But there's no room!"

"Fine," said Lapouille calmly, "not another word. I'll sleep at the hotel."

"The guardhouse for *men* is full. We'll put you in the NCO guardhouse. There's nobody there at the moment."

But Lapouille would have nothing of it. He objected coolly:

"Excuse me, sir, but I am a *man*, and I intend to receive my punishment in the guardhouse for *men*."

"But I told you: it's full, you idiot!"

"I don't care, sir. I am a *man*, and that's all I know!"

"But, you imbecile, you'll be better off in the non-com guardhouse!"

"This is not a question of my comfort! This is a question of principle. Am I a *man*? I am. Well, then! I should be put in the guardhouse for *men*. When I become a sergeant, you can put me in the NCO guardhouse, and I won't say a word. But for now... I am a *man*."

By this time, the sergeant, impatient with the interchange, suggested seizing Lapouille by the shoulders, and throwing him into the *clink* with a good kick in the behind. Lapouille then assumed a grave expression.

"Sir, I am in my rights. If you assault me, I will write to the *French Republic*."

Why the *French Republic*, and not some other paper? Nobody ever knew. But it was Lapouille's crowning argument: as soon as a corporal assigned him a task too brusquely, Lapouille immediately threatened to write to the *French Republic*.

At this menace, the sergeant's face fell. Damn! The *French Republic*!

And Lapouille continued, implacable:

"I am a *man*. That's all I know! I am a *man*! I want a cell for *men*!"

Finally, he was sent back to his own bed.

The name stuck: we no longer said *Lapouille*, we said the *Man*; the *Man* here, the *Man* there.

This exploit indicates the character of my friend Lapouille, the type of soldier who always gets what he wants, the kind that the army fittingly calls: *one who doesn't want to know.*

No, Lapouille didn't want to know — not about exercises, not about duties, not about discipline.

"But you just don't give a damn!" the captain said to him one day.

"No, sir," Lapouille replied politely, "not in the least."

And he developed, for the sake of his laziness and serenity, superb techniques of inertia, of looking like an incurable idiot, of genial cunning, and, above all, of such imperturbability, such indifference to military discipline, such foolish oblivion (apparently, at any rate), that his superiors dared not punish him; and he often netted two days of confinement for some infraction that would have sent any of his comrades off to hard labor in Africa.

The Damoclesism of his famous *French Republic* earned him special treatment from both corporals and sergeants, stout fellows for whom fear of the press is the beginning of wisdom.

Around Christmas, Lapouille did like the others, and requested permission to visit Paris for a week, to restore himself in the bosom of his family.

Lapuouille did not get his wish, his previous conduct making him ineligible for approval.

Our friend showed no disappointment and raised no protest, but, I can assure you that at evening assembly on Christmas day, when the corporal called out Lapouille, nobody answered; for the excellent reason that Lapouille was in Paris, swigging mulled wine with a few of his friends.

The little party lasted six days.

Young Lapouille seemed to have as little concern for his regiment as for his first pair of galoshes. He had found a little girlfriend and some jolly companions, and had wangled some money from his family. Time passed merrily.

On the evening of the sixth day, as he was dining in joyful company, a friend who had already *served* turned to him, during dessert, and said:

"You don't seem worried, old pal, but this evening you'll be reported as a deserter."

Despite his contempt for military regulations, Lapouille felt an unpleasant chill... Deserter!

He had a brief and disturbing vision of the Bat' d'Af', of silos, of stones broken along unshaded roads.

In a word, Lapouille stopped having fun.

He finished his dinner, spent the evening with his friends, and retired discreetly at about eleven.

Twenty minutes later, he was at the Place Vendôme, and hailed the sentry for the Military Governorship of Paris.

"Good evening, my friend. Nasty weather, eh?"

The sentry, a serious lad, made no reply. Lapouille persisted.

"Does the Governor of Paris live here?"

"Yes, this is the place."

"Well, go tell him that I wish to speak with him."

"Say, are you crazy, wanting to talk to the Governor of Paris at this time of night?"

"Don't you worry about that, old man. Go tell him that I wish to speak with him, right away."

"You'd be better off going home to bed. You're drunk, you'll just get yourself in trouble."

"You won't go get the Governor of Paris? Once, twice..."

"Hell, no!"

"Fine, I'll go myself."

And since Lapouille seemed determined to enter, the sentry had to bar the way with his bayonet and call for a guard.

"Sergeant," said Lapouille, "go tell the Governor of Paris that there's someone down here who wishes to speak with him."

They tried to negotiate with Lapouille, to reason with him, to send him home to bed. Nothing worked. Lapouille would not give up; he insisted on seeing the Governor of Paris.

One officer, drawn by the commotion, finally lost his patience:

"Throw that man in a cell. We'll see tomorrow."

The next day, at the break of dawn, the station rang with Lapouille's demands.

"The Governor of Paris! The Governor of Paris! I have something very important to communicate to the Governor of Paris."

Maybe it was true, after all. And besides, what did they have to lose?

Thus, the Governor of Paris called Lapouille into his office.

"You're the one that insists on seeing me, my friend? What's this all about?"

"It's like this, sir: My colonel sent me to Paris to polish the dome of the Invalides. Now, I forgot my tripoli, and don't have the money to buy another one. So, I come to ask you either to furnish me with a tripoli, or to send me back to my regiment to get mine."

This little speech was delivered in such a serious tone, that Lapouille, with all the respect due to his rank, was escorted to the Val-de-Grâce, after a rather brief delay.

There, he did not yield one iota. He repeated for the doctors his story about polishing the dome of the Invalides, his lack of tripoli, and his fear of being *caught* by his colonel.

He was put *under observation*. A month later, he was cured.

From time to time, I run into good old Lapouille, and he never fails to remark:

"Did you ever see such a pack of idiots?"

BUSINESS CAFE

The scene takes place in a large cafe on the boulevard. A mixed crowd.

A group of journalists bitterly debate the future of the French press. Some claim that what the public needs is this and that. Others insist, with remarkable conviction, that no, the public demands something else, and now must be given something other than this and that, or... And they come to no conclusion.

A few suburban couples consult the listings and times for shows. At the title of each play, the little wife (not very well dressed, but rather pretty) makes a face:

"Isn't there anything by Gandillot?" she asks.

The husband returns to the listings and confirms, poor fellow, that no, there isn't anything by Gandillot.

At the next table, a young woman seems to be impatiently waiting for someone, without knowing exactly whom (in my opinion).

On the other side, a heavy gentleman in an astrakhan collar orders, with a peremptory air, an *absinthe with sugar* and *pen and paper.*

"Ah, there you are!" he declares to a tall young man, pale, with pimples, who has just entered.

"Yes, sir, here I am!" replies the poor tall young man, in a voice as pale as his face.

"Did you see that person?"

"I just left her."

"What did she say?"

"She said that she couldn't decide anything until she had *chatted* with that individual."

"And the individual, what did he do today?"

"Well, he went to see that lady in Versailles."

"Why would he do that, go see the lady in Versailles?"

"Because the good woman won't spend a sou without the advice of that notary in Etampe."

"That notary in Etampe is starting to give us trouble! Just last week, he told that fellow that it was a done deal."

"Yes, except that guy saw the fellow since then."

During this exchange, the tall pale young man, with pimples, seems to be waiting for the gentleman in the astrakhan collar to ask *what he will have.*

Given the gentleman's silence (deliberate or inadvertent?) the poor pale young man orders a *bitter mint.*

The conversation then takes a less general turn, and I learn that it concerns a sum to be raised to develop a marvelous invention, the *chrysoscope*, which can find, unfailingly and from afar, the smallest vein of gold. An exciting opportunity!

Except, well! It's not going as planned. The *person* missed her meeting with the *individual*, who was not able to see the *guy*. On the other hand, the *guy* had a mix-up with the *lady in Versailles.* The notary in Etampe, throughout the whole business, is acting like a nincompoop.

As for the *colonel*, it's none too clear what the *colonel* has to do with all of this. Indeed!

And the gentleman in the astrakhan collar remarks, not without bitterness, that the world has certainly changed, in the last ten years...!

The cafe empties.

People go off to dinner.

Only the table with the two *businessmen* shows any sign of life.

"Well, what do you know, there's that *guy!*"

He's a good one, that guy!

He's the kind of shabby old Bohemian who must have been a lot of laughs back in 1867, but who has gone downhill since then.

From time to time, he gets by on his reputation as a brilliant inventor, in whom even *persons* and *individuals* sometimes want to invest.

"Well!" says the astrakhan collar. "Did you finally bring your famous *chrysoscope?*"

"Oh, my poor friends! What an adventure I've had!... Just imagine, as I passed the Bank of France, on rue Vivienne, the needle on my invention went crazy. I started running, to get my machine away from all that gold. Unfortunately, it was too late... No sooner had I reached the corner of rue Colbert than my poor device fell into pieces!"

The funniest part of the story is that the brilliant inventor of the *chrysoscope* wept in earnest, and that both businessmen felt pearling, in their usually dry eyes, furtive tears.

TOO MANY KANGAROOS

At the present time, Paris — if I count correctly — holds within its borders no fewer than three boxing kangaroos.[1]

The number three, which would be insignificant were we enumerating stars in the firmament, or grains of sand in the desert, acquires a special importance when the census of kangaroos is the subject.

For a long time, Paris was bereft of boxing kangaroos. We found ourselves no worse, and no better, for that matter.

One came to the Nouveau-Cirque.

Then the Folies-Bergères offered a second.

Today, it is the turn of the Casino de Paris, which announces a third in the not too distant future.

The boxing kangaroo — let us not pretend otherwise — is all the rage.

I thought that it would be interesting to look into the causes for this movement.

And who better to ask than the kangaroos themselves? That is what I did.

Kangaroos are not represented in Paris by any ambassador, by any consul. Not even a chargé d'affaires!

And yet they comprise, in the capital, two important colonies.

The first, modest and a bit tainted with nihilism — or so I am told — lives in the neighborhood of the Jardin des Plantes.

The other, composed of somewhat more settled individuals, has chosen to reside in the Bois de Boulogne, in the Jardin d'acclimatation, to be be precise.

It was the latter that I went to see.

Although it was still early, those gentlemen had already arisen, and were jumping gaily around the large park elegantly designed for them by M. Geoffroy Saint-Hilaire, the well-known dog breeder.

The first ones that I contacted were little frivolous kangaroos, with short attention spans. Besides, having been born in Neuilly, those little quadrupeds could have given me only insignificant leads.

Luckily, an adult came out of his shack at that moment. He saw me, and approached in a series of leaps.

After the introductions:

"I know what brings you here," said the wise kangaroo. "You would like my opinion on those of our colleagues who exhibit themselves, every evening, in the circuses and music halls of Paris."

"Exactly!"

"Very well, sir, since you have the honor of holding a pen, you can say that all of us, all serious kangaroos worthy of the name, consider our boxing brothers merely tramps and clowns."

And since this indignant outburst had fatigued him, the old kangaroo drew his little paw across his little forehead, and wiped away a few little drops of sweat. He continued:

"We belong, sir, to an old family, with an honorable reputation throughout Australia, the family of Marsupials. None of us, until the present, ever dreamed of taking to the stage nightly, with ridiculous routines, in some place of pleasure. To what may we attribute this orgy of boxing kangaroos? At first, I thought it was a defense of our reputation: naturalists, blathering about the disproportionate dimensions between our heads, our apparently frail anterior members, and our hindquarters, composed of two impressive feet and a tail that needs no description, had insinuated that our forequarters suffered from a sort of atrophy, which is false, sir, and you can tell that to your readers. Had a few of our brothers decided to prove the contrary? That was what I assumed at first. Alas! Nothing of the kind with those gentlemen!"

The old kangaroo pulled from his pouch a few olives, which he nibbled while bracing himself with his tail.

"But then," I insinuated...

"The urge to strut upon the stage affects all the beings in creation. Kangaroos are no more immune than any others. And they are even stupider, those imbeciles, because they work for free. (I've seen their contracts.) Neither paid nor clothed. They're furnished with food, lodging, and boxing gloves, and that's it."

Visibly indignant, the old kangaroo shrugged his shoulders.

"Obviously," I remarked, "with such a regimen, the marsupial boxers will never enjoy your sprightly old age."

"Oh, I owe my health to my old habit of eating olives. Every morning, my friend, the poet Jean Sarrazin, brings me a small supply, which I nibble all day, following the old principle of the school of Salerno:

He who feeds himself on olive,
In all seasons, and all weather
Will last longer far than all of
Our old houses put together."

And with this quatrain, perhaps not particularly authentic, the old kangaroo took his leave, returning to his shack in a series of bounds.

And I retired, quite moved by what I had heard, murmuring mechanically:

He who feeds himself on all of
Our old houses put together... etc.

————

1. Since the author wrote these lines, there has been a considerable lull. The boxing kangaroo has emigrated toward other skies.

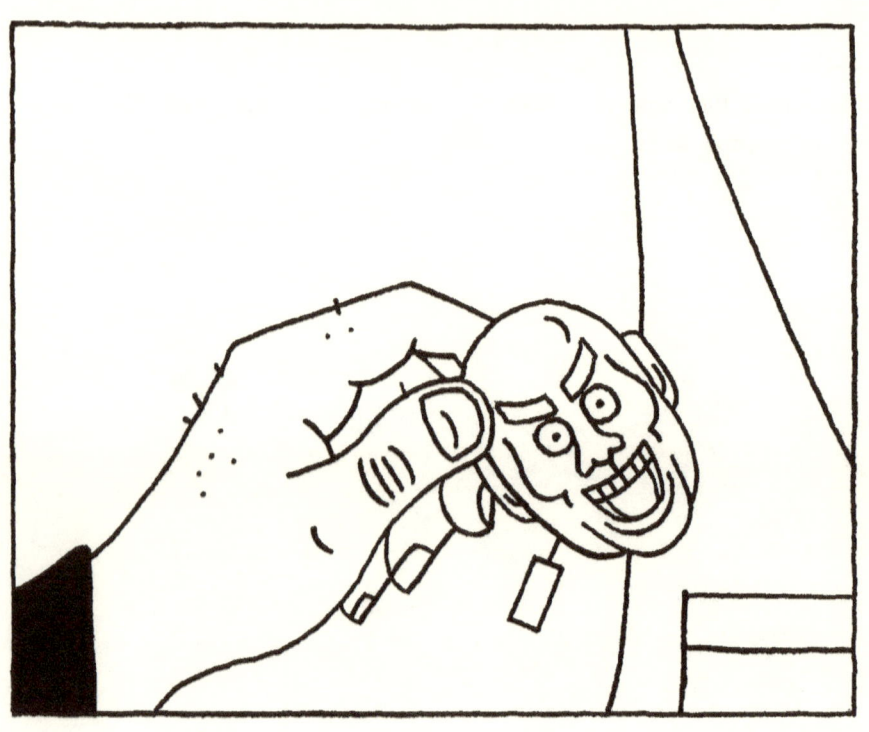

A PLEASANT MEMORY

When I was a student, and had no money to go to the cafe, it was in department stores like the Louvre or the Bon-Marché that I spent the majority of my afternoons.

None was as skilled as I at insinuating myself into the best part of the crowd.

None could be elbowed—I say *elbowed* for the sake of politeness—by customers who were more vivacious, more buxom, or of firmer consistency.

And even today, despite the important position that I hold in Paris, despite the responsibilities that fall on me like autumn leaves, despite constant orders from the provinces and overseas, I am not too proud to spend, in some Calicopolis, an occasional half-hour or two.

And besides, it brings back memories.

Let me tell you a story (I am dying to).

It was quite a while ago, which does not make me any younger. I had conceived an ardent passion for a young employee at the Louvre.

She was not extraordinarily pretty, but her black eyes, which glittered gold at times, and where, deep down, Enigma crouched; the curls that encumbered her youthful brow; her frank and cheerful nose; her mouth that was too large, but so splendidly furnished; all gave her such a funny little air!

A casual observer could not have said if she came from Benares or rue Lepic (in the eighteenth arrondissement).

Every day, I appeared at her counter, and, as a pretext for a bit of a chat, acquired a few objects at a moderate price.

Which objects, incidentally, I quietly returned the next day, as if they had suddenly ceased to please me.

Things were not going badly, when an older gentleman, quite smitten with my kitten from Montmartre, caused a decline in my activity.

This elderly man was rich, amiable, and copious with his promises.

In short, I decided to play one of those little tricks which prevents a gentlemen from setting foot again in an establishment.

One fine day, I slipped into his overcoat pocket a small Japanese ivory, previously swiped by myself, and denounced him to a policeman.

The poor man was invited to visit the station *ad hoc*. He had to sign compromising papers, and pay an enormous fine.

I never saw him again at the Louvre, but — alas! — nor did I see the young woman who made my heart beat so.

The day after the incident, the gentleman sent for her through a third party, laden with gold.

This adventure taught me a lesson, and since that day, I have never stuffed a single Japanese ivory into an elderly gentleman's pocket.

FIRE

I once heard, a while ago, a story that I found quite amusing.

A gentleman died after having requested that his body be cremated.

When the *ad hoc* employee asked the widow what kind of cremation she wanted for the deceased (French or Milanese oven?), she cried, "Oh, sir, the French oven! My husband hated the smell of Italian cooking."

I was reminded of this fine example of conjugal piety when I learned that a committee for the improvement of cremations was active in the Prefecture of the Seine.

The composition of the committee is not without interest: physicians are in the majority, Dr. Bourneville, Dr. Martin, Dr. Napias, etc.

Why all these doctors?

I understand that they value their clientele, but keeping their interest up to the moment of combustion seems unpleasantly insistent. Too much zeal, gentlemen!

The objections made to cremation, as practiced today, are rather picturesque.

For example, the regulations at Père-Lachaise authorize only five members of the funeral party to attend the operation.

Why this rigorous exclusivity for a performance that will not be repeated, and which had no dress rehearsal?

And among the five witnesses, only one has the right to follow, through a special peephole reserved for employees, the progress of the incineration.

Does this single viewer constitute a serious control?

And besides, why have a control? Are they worried that the

administration will abscond with the cadaver? What would it do with it, I ask you?

While the privileged five warm themselves at the grate of the late (not bad that, by the way), the other guests go off to kill time around the columbarium. And then what happens? The wind brings them smoke that does not come exclusively from coal.

An extremely disagreeable sensation! For, after all, just because a gentleman got up your nose when he was alive is no reason to keep inhaling him after his demise.

Other painful details will be avoided in the future.

The committee is elaborating plans for decent, even sumptuous, funerals.

The idea of transforming the departed into briquettes, to heat the family, has been definitively rejected.

All the same, what a strange idea to mix all of those doctors into the story!

The next time that I become ill, I will certainly not consult Dr. Napias.

I would be too tempted to remark:

"With that one, I'm toast!"

IT WAS SNOWING...!
OR THE OSTINATION [SIC] OF A CYCLIST

A page of drawings for Caran d'Ache

I

It was snowing...! Bleak plain! to quote Victor Hugo, one of the lads of his epoch who had the best pipelines to bleak plains.

Nevertheless, the intrepid cyclist straddles his steel mount and heads in the direction of the horizon, a bit to the right.

II

The snow, for all that, does not cease to fall. It blurs with its white pencil the man's hooded silhouette, sprinkles the soil.

The wheels turn, and the tires, with each rotation, become a bit more encumbered (the story of the snowball).

III

Continuation of the preceding, with augmentation.

White plains give way to more white plains, again quoting the aforementioned Papa Hugo.

The cyclist pedals, undiscourageable.

IV

Meanwhile, the situation worsens.

The cyclist's hooded silhouette is barely recognizable beneath the snowfall which envelops him.

The periphery — if you will excuse the expression — of the Dunlops has accumulated so much snow that the wheels are not far from tangent.

A wan smile on his lips, the cyclist keeps going, devouring space as an elephant might a five centime loaf of rye bread.

V

It is done.

The two enlarged wheels now touch one another. Nothing works any more.

As for the man, who would guess that he is a man?

And yet, the cyclist still strains his useless muscles against the inert pedals.

The storm takes the opportunity to redouble in severity.

VI

The athlete and his implement have become an amorphous group, where even the most practiced eye could discern no trace of man or machine.

The little birds contemplate the thing, wide-eyed with amazement.

It was snowing...!

(Thaw next issue.)

ON THE DISADVANTAGES OF EXCESSIVE BAUDELAIREISM

We must have Baudelaire, of course, but we must not have too much. The following anecdote will demonstrate, for the intelligent part of my clientele, what we should take from Baudelaireism, and what we should leave behind.

A tall blond young man, with a soul of azure, was a student at an excellent pharmacy in Paris. His time was spent between his pharmaceutical preoccupations and reading, obsessively, *The Flowers of Evil.*

Not a word murmured near him; not an image evoked; not a nothing at all, in fact, which did not instantly trigger a line or two from General Apick's divine stepson.

One day a woman entered the pharmacy, and said to him:

"We have just bottled some wine, my husband and I, but the bottom of the cask is terribly murky, and I have come for a filter."

The young student gave her a filter.

Either the filter was made of some truly unresistant material, or the woman poured the liquid too brusquely, for it broke.

And the woman returned to the pharmacy, saying to the young man:

"Would you have a stronger filter?"

Suddenly prompted by her words, the young Baudelairean declaimed:

The strongest philtres one can take
Can never match your slothfulness,
For you know every strange caress
To spur the sleeping dead to wake!

Legitimately offended by this hectoring quatrain, which she did not deserve, and which, we might add, she certainly did not expect, the woman went to report the thing to her husband, who lost no time in giving the ethereal student a sound beating.

Was I not right to say in the beginning: We must have Baudelaireism, of course, but we must not have too much?

THE BULLET BABY

I begin by declaring before the world that the following story did not emerge, quivering, from my febrile imagination.

I cannot guarantee its authenticity, and, to tell the truth, find it rather hard to swallow.

But I cite my sources: the incident in question was published in an issue of the *Hospital Gazette*, which claimed that it found it in *The Lancet*, in London, which *Lancet* had borrowed it from *The American Medical Weekly*.

Now that I have discharged my duty (nothing saddens me more than not being taken seriously), I can tell the story:

It was in America, during the Civil War.

On May 12, 1863, two enemy corps encountered one another, and waged a fierce battle, near a sumptuous villa occupied by a woman and her two daughters.

At the height of the action, a young combatant, stationed 150 meters from the house, had his leg fractured by a bullet from a Minié rifle, which, and this is an important detail, also carried off part of an organ which is difficult to name more clearly, an organ which counts seriously in a man's life.

At the same time, a piercing cry echoed throughout the sumptuous villa occupied by the woman and the two young ladies. One of these last, the elder, had just been shot in the abdomen.

The entrance wound was about midway between the umbilicus and the anterior spinal process of the ilium. A penetrating wound, with no issue.

After various adventures too long to recount here, the two injured patients healed: the young woman, in her room at home; the soldier, in the ambulance, a few leagues from the sumptuous villa.

Keep in mind that the lady and gentleman did not know each other *even by the lips or teeth*, as my concierge puts it.

The young miss suffered a peritonitis, leaving her with a swollen abdomen, which worried her.

Exactly two hundred seventy-eight days after the injury, sharp pains began, and the interesting patient put into the world a fine eight pound boy.

The family was understandably upset.

As for the miss, the entire experience was, as we say in France, like finding a hair in her soup.

Three weeks later, the newborn was operated on for a congenital tumor in his scrotum.

Dr. Capers, who strikes me as a fellow not easily surprised, was stunned to discover that the child's tumor was caused by a Minié bullet, which was crushed and deformed, as if it had struck something hard in its trajectory.

Suddenly, a light went on in his brain! We shall let him speak, stopping him only when he becomes too technically precise:

"What is there to say? The bullet that I extracted from the child's scrotum was the same which, on May 12, had broken my young friend's tibia, carrying away with it... etc., etc."

Exactly!

At any rate, the intrepid yankee soldier, apprised of the situation, married the young woman, and gave her three children: none of which, Dr. Capers tells us, resembled him as much as the first.

In America, when there is no more, there is still more!

It would be excessive to draw from this story the moral that the old system of reproduction should give way to the American system.

The case cited here was successful, but it could have failed, and damn! that would have been some failure, eh?

THE AWAKENING OF 22

This Monday morning, I had a good laugh, and I mean a good laugh! And when I think back on it, I laugh again.

I had spent Sunday in Versailles, with some of my most debauched companions.

The day was calm, but the evening did not pass without the filthiest orgies. Lust and intemperance combined!

So much, and so well, that I missed, imperturbably, the last train to Paris.

A great indecision overtook me: should I return to the houses of ill repute whence I came, or spend the night bourgeoisely in some peaceful little hotel?

My guardian angel breathed upon my brow, dissipating the devil's evil inspirations, and there I was on the path of virtue.

The hotel clerk, roused no doubt from some dream of riches, gave me a welcome not exactly sparkling with enthusiasm.

He announced, nevertheless, that I would occupy room twenty-one.

I forgot to tell you that it was enormously important that I be back in Paris early the next day. But this omission is of no importance, since I still have time to apprise you of this detail.

In the hotel office hung a blackboard, upon which the guests wrote the times at which they wished to be awakened.

I have always had a horror of sudden awakenings. Therefore, long ago I adopted the habit of writing, not my own room number, but those of my two collaterals.

For example: I occupy 21; I write, to be awakened at a given time, 20 and 22.

In this way, my awakening is less brusque.

(A technique especially recommended for more high-strung travelers.)

The night that I spent in that inn was quiet, and populated with the sweetest dreams.

At the break of day, fearsome growling uprooted me from my slumber.

A loud voice, redolent of the roar of the bear and the song of the polecat, grumbled:

"What? Leave me the hell alone! What do I care if it's six thirty? Idiot!"

It was 20 upbraiding the clerk for awakening him against his will.

Me, I laughed so hard that I almost split my sides.

For 22, the thing was even more epic.

The clerk knocked on the door: tap, tap, tap.

"Eh?" said 22. "Who is it?"

"It's six thirty, sir."

"Ah!"

The clerk withdrew.

I glued my ear to the wall that separated me from 22, and I heard this last murmuring in a miserable voice, "Six thirty! Six thirty! What was I supposed to do this morning?"

Then, the unfortunate man arose, made his toilette, and dressed, still muttering to himself, "Six thirty! Six thirty! What the devil was I supposed to do this morning?"

He left the hotel at the same time as me.

He was a man of peaceful mien, but whose usual mansuetude was tinged, for the moment, with a touch of concern.

I hurried to the station, but not without looking back, from time to time, at my poor 22.

He gazed up at the firmament with a discouraged air, and I guessed, from the movement of his lips, that he was saying, "What the devil was I supposed to do this morning? Six thirty!"

Poor 22!

A FEW NUMBERS

Terront emerged victorious in the race known as the *Terront-Corre Race*, having *covered* one thousand kilometers in 41 hours, 68 minutes, and 52 4/5 seconds.

A parenthesis, please.

(Some of my uninitiated readers have written from the provinces to ask that I shed light on this expression *covered*. Why do we say *he covered*, rather than *he rode*?

The explanation is rather interesting.

It was M. Porel, the intelligent former director of the Eden, whose real name is Rhodes, who convinced the cycling authorities to replace the word *rode* with the word *covered*, to avoid any regrettable confusion.

Close the parenthesis, please.)

Since I had nothing to do this morning, I indulged in a few calculations.

1000 kilometers in 41 hours, 68 minutes, and 52 4/5 seconds comes to one kilometer in 19 seconds and 12 tierces (the tierce is a unit of measurement seldom used in daily life, corresponding to a sixtieth of a second), and one meter in 1 tierce and something.

I didn't figure the millimeter, as the calculation seemed pointless. One would have to be rather bizarre, after all, to try for the millimeter record.

This impressive speed, quite respectable for a cyclist, becomes almost laughable when we compare it to the speed of light (77,000 leagues a second).

It should be mentioned that light has been training every instant since the first days of creation (which does not make it any younger), whereas Terront took up the bicycle only fifteen years ago.

Theoretically, Terront could go around the world in seventy days. (Take that, my old Jules Verne!)

In practice, this should be adjusted, the surface of the globe being appreciably rougher than the track at the Vélodrame at the Champ de Mars.

And, while we're on the subject, allow me to express a request that will find an echo in the hearts of all record-holders.

Now that there are no more stagecoaches or mailcoaches, the major roads of France have lost that lively animation that once made them so picturesque.

Even highway robbers have disappeared: some, used to the open air, now exercise the profession of pickpocket at the racetrack; others have taken up merchant banking.

The increased popularity of cycling has returned our national roads to their former level of activity.

Cannot the General Council of Roads and Bridges maintain our thoroughfares in a fashion better suited to bicycles?

Gravel. freshly crushed, is excellent for the wheels of trucks or wagons, but worthless for the rubber tires of our vehicles, absolutely worthless.

Ah, if I were the government!

FRENCH RABBITS AND BELGIAN FROGS

Credible explorers told me, some time ago, that the art of German cooking consists of cooking rabbit with jam.

I don't know if rabbits, like hares, who love so to be skinned alive, adore sweets, but they will have to get used to them, if I am to believe the last meeting of the Academy of Sciences.

The few scattered rabbits — you could have counted them — who attended this meeting of the great scholarly body were distressed to hear an announcement from M. Chauveau, an announcement which was unprovoked, I might add, and could not have been foreseen:

"M. Hédou, of Montpellier, said M. Chauveau, has succeeded in making rabbits diabetic, by destroying the pancreas with the Claude Bernard method, that is, by injecting olive oil into the excretory duct."

Before the astonishment had completely abated, M. Chauveau added calmly:

"This development permits physiologists to obtain, in little time, by a simple operation (for the physiologists, that is) a large number of diabetic rabbits."

It's as simple as that. You would like to rabbit away with a young woman of recent acquaintance. A little olive oil in the excretory duct, suppression of the pancreas, and there you have a little sugared rabbit that will pass like a letter through the mail.

We will no longer say *sugar the pill,* but *sweeten the rabbit,* which is far more elegant.

Ah! Poor rabbits of France!

How I prefer the new destiny that awaits Belgian frogs!

By dint of demanding a king, the frogs have found one, and a good one at that.

For once, you must know, I refer to Leopold!... who will bear, throughout history, the honored title of *father of all frogs*.

The reason for this sudden tenderness towards batrachians? Ah, please, do not insist. I haven't a clue.

I wrote to Belgium to find out. If I learn anything, I'll drop you a line.

While waiting, I submit for your grazing the first two articles of a circular addressed by the chief engineer of the Northern Railway to those of his agents who conduct trains into France, and which calls their attention to the following royal decree:

Art. 1: It is forbidden, effective from this date, throughout the country, to catch or to destroy frogs, to transport, display for purchase, buy, or sell these animals, either whole or in part. However, the proprietors of frog farms situated in districts designated by the minister may send, under conditions and at times determined by him, and only into another country, nonliving frogs, either in whole or in part.

Art. 2: The minister may also, in the interests of science or public welfare, authorize special dispensation of the provisions in the first paragraph of the preceding article.

And yet, even as I pay tribute to Leopold's great heart, that second article chills me.

What if some Belgian scientist got it into his head to make frogs albuminuric!

Perhaps sometime in the future — and sooner than you think, Madame — we will eat meringues in which the egg whites are furnished by frogs, and the sugar by rabbits.

It is the vegetarians who will be most upset!

A GLOOMY POEM

Translated from the Belgian

For Maeterlinck

Without being old, she whom I would love would be of a certain age.
She would have seen everything, and believed nothing.
Not beautiful, but convinced that she bewitched all men, without
exception.
Nobody would have seen her laugh.
Her pale lips would infrequently display the heartbreaking smile of
her disappointments.

Former mistress of an English painter, a violent drunk
who would have bruised her body,
all of her body,
with his fists,
she would have conceived a fierce hatred for all men.

She would be unfaithful to me with a young unpublished poet,
whose abundant, long,
and indifferently kempt hair
would turn the heads of pedestrians
and pedestriennes.

I would know, but, craven, would prefer to know nothing.

Nothing!
However, I would take the proper precautions.
The young poet would dedicate his productions to me,
ironically.

★

This thing would go on for months
and months.
Then, one fine day, Eloa would take to morphine.

★

For her name would be Eloa.

★

The morphine would do its work,
its evil work.
Eloa's face would become white, swollen,
so swollen that one could not see her eyes,
and speckled with blackheads.
She would stop eating.
For hours at a time, she would lie on her canopy,
like a great weary beast.
And fetid odors would mingle with the vapors of her breath.

★

One day when Eloa's pharmacist was drunk,
he would make a mistake,
and instead of morphine,

give her some powerful alkaloid.
Eloa would become sick,
as sick as a horse.
Her extremities would turn cold,
like a serpent's,
and all of the sufferings of constriction
would rendezvous in her chest.

☆

The agony would begin.

☆

My hand in hers,
Eloa would have me swear
that when she was dead,
I would kill myself.
Our two bodies, enclosed in the same tomb,
would decompose into a common purulence.
The combined liquor of our putrefying corpses would pass into the
same sap,
would produce the same wood in the same bushes,
would spread, viridian, into the same leaves,
would blossom out into the same flowers.

☆

And, in the cemetery,
in springtime,
when a young woman would exclaim: *What a sweet aroma!*
that aroma would be, commingled, our two sublimated souls.

This would be Eloa's final request.
I would promise her everything she wanted, and more as well.

★

Eloa would die.

★

I would give Eloa a proper funeral, and,
the next day,
find another mistress
who is more fun.

EXCESS IN ANYTHING IS A FAULT

A KANAK STORY

Yesterday, in the course of the afternoon, I went to see the Dahomeyans at the Champ-de-Mars.

I was accompanied by a former sea captain, whom I had not seen for some time, and had just met, that morning, at the funeral of one of my cousins.

The Dahomeyans and Dahomeyennes enchanted me.

There may be some among them, of course, who have yet to discover how to detonate ammonium picrate, but one can see it in their eyes, which gleam with sly and malicious intelligence.

"Did you ever travel in those regions?" I asked my friend.

"When I was young, yes, a bit, but I rarely disembarked. What I'm more familiar with are the Kanaks. They're nasty, those Kanaks! And clever!"

"Ah!"

"You have no idea of those rascals! And what contempt they have for us Europeans, deep down!"

"Ah!"

"I remember one day... Ah, how they made me laugh!"

"Tell me, captain."

"My ship was in dry dock. A whole week with nothing to do. I walked around the island, all alone, with devilish nerve; but when you know how to take them, they're not too dangerous, those fellows. The weather was frightful, a real tempest!

"One day, I saw, sitting on a large rock, a dozen Kanaks who seemed to be amusing themselves enormously. Here is what comprised those gentlemen's entertainment: a poor wretch of a European was in the water, swimming desperately for shore, and the Kanaks were coming to his rescue with the rather special technique of violently throwing pebbles at his head.

"The poor man seemed to be at the end of his rope. I brutally intervened: with the help of a few punches to the face and kicks in the behind, judiciously distributed, I introduced some sentiments of Christian charity into the hearts of those brutes. Holding hands, they formed a chain, and pulled the unlucky fellow from the lemonade.

"He was a poor devil of an English sailor, who had been swept from the deck of his schooner by a wave, and who, with great effort, had just managed to swim to shore.

"I suggested that the Kanaks take care of him, that they warm him and dry him out, etc., and continued on my way.

"Several hours later, returning to the place, my nose was tickled deliciously by the exquisite aroma of roasting.

"Well, I thought, some folks over there must be having a nice little cookout.

"I took a few steps and saw, on the rocks, my Kanaks around a fire, where they were grilling... guess what!... the poor limey we had just saved.

"As you can imagine, I unleashed all the curses in my repertory! Then, one of the Kanaks left the group, and said to me, in a tone I shall never forget: Hell, you're the one that told us to dry him out!"

A TRUE PEARL

Around the beginning of this month, the young Viscount Guy de Neucoulant felt his poor soul invaded with melancholy.

His mistress had left him.

Why had his mistress left him?

Would you like to know? You don't care? Well, what about me, then?

Well, I'll tell you anyway, even though it's not of excessive interest.

It's not particularly dirty, but will do for now.

Hortense — need I mention that her name was Hortense? — was a delectable individual, as beautiful as the dawn, but as simple as the moon.

The ease with which this young woman fell for the most outrageous lies was truly prodigious.

Ah! She didn't invent melinite (and, in passing, let us regret it, for M. Turpin's sake). However, once she realized that she'd been fooled, she resented it fiercely, and the goose changed into a hyena.

It was this susceptibility that led to the rupture mentioned above.

One day when she and Guy were in some American bar (the one on rue Volney, maybe), she noticed a newspaper left on a table. The newspaper was called *The Shipping Gazette*. She asked Guy what the name meant.

"What?" Guy asked in surprise. "You don't know?"

"My stars, no."

"It's a paper for pickpockets. In English, picking pockets is called *shipping*. In fact, that's where we get the French word *chiper*."

"You don't say."

"Well, I'm telling you."

"Those pickpockets have their nerve, putting out their own paper! And the police, what do they say about this?"

"They know all about it, but they can't do anything."

That evening, Hortense dined with friends, and had nothing better to do than tell the story of the journal for crooks.

The other guests didn't have enough hands to hold their sides.

Hortense understood, and the next morning left for Menton, accompanied by a rich American sugarer, Mr. Gabriell Bonnett, director of the *Oxnard Beet Sugar Company, Grand Island, Nebraska* (U. S. A.), who had long and avidly pursued her.

The poor Viscount Guy de Neucoulant was as miserable as sin, but you must admit that he had it coming to him.

As a final irony, Hortense left this simple note, which was, for her, rather clever:

"My dear friend,

"If you want to know why I left you, read the next issue of *The Dumping Gazette.*"

But enough of this Hortense, who was, after all, a bit of a tart, and let us proceed to other exercises.

Guy had long been solicited by his aunt, the Marquise of Pertuissec, to go hunting on the lands that would one day be his.

Without hesitation, he took the 10:57 train (to be precise), and arrived that evening at his worthy relative's home.

A cordial reception, hello my nephew, hello my aunt, you look a bit tired, you look quite well, what news from Paris, etc.

The Marquise, who, in her day, seldom spat on love, had become extremely severe with age.

She willingly forgot those halcyon times, in which her poor puny Marquis resembled one of those little Sengalese oxen, as fat as two pats of butter, and with horns that seemed to stab the sky.

The chateau of Pertuissec had become a citadel of virtue.

Everyone vied to be more virtuous, from the stable boys to the austere headwaiter.

Above all, the female domestics were remarkable in this respect, and it was quite frustrating, thought Guy, because, damn! what lovely ladies!

At breakfast, Guy could not help mentioning it.

"Congratulations, my aunt, on that little chambermaid of yours. She's not the kind of flower you'd just want to put in a vase."

"And why would you put her in a vase?" the Marquise asked, not without a touch of disapproval.

When she understood, the Marquise extolled the moral qualities of her servant, adding:

"A pearl, my friend, a true pearl!"

Within the park, across the snow,
Two spectral forms pass to and fro.

.....

I'll cut the quotation from Verlaine short, since the rest would not be in keeping with the spirit of this story.

Those forms, in fact, did not have dead eyes, their lips were not slack, and if one hardly heard their words, it was because they had replaced conversation with lively and vigorous pantomime.

One of those forms — you've already guessed, unless you're grossly stupid — was named Guy de Neucoulant.

The other belonged to a pretty little chambermaid, a pearl, a true pearl!

It was to the hothouse that they were headed.

Pale Phoebus, scandalized by the spectacle, covered her eyes with thick gray clouds.

Let us do as she.

Guy had not completely finished demonstrating to his partner that she should not be put in a vase, when the hothouse door opened.

A spectral form portrayed by the Marquise of Pertuissec came forward:

No doubt about it.

The Viscount was as red as a rooster (a red rooster, naturally).

The maid displayed approximately the same color, but somewhat lighter. Moreover, her hair was mussed down to the marrow of her bones.

With a withering gaze, the Marquise contemplated the scene of carnage.

Sheepishly, Guy brushed off his knees—the customary gesture on such occasions—and stammered vague and foolish excuses:

"Well, my aunt, you know what they say about casting the first stone."

The Marquise responded icily:

"And, my boy, about casting pearls before swine."

SCIENCE AIDED BY POLITICAL AMBITION WORKS MIRACLES

A plan for a decorative mural for the School of Medicine

"What, is that you?"

"Damnation!" the gentleman answered calmly. "Yes, it is! Unless it's the Burgomaster of Brussels, or Prince Oscar of Sweden..."

"All right, it's you; but how you've changed! *Quantum mutatis* itself could not have changed as much as you at this moment... So, you're feeling better?"

"I'm not feeling better, I'm feeling fine. Cured, old man, cured! Have you ever been cured?"

"More often than I deserve, my poor friend. And how were you cured, and by whom?"

"Oh! There's a story to make you roll on the ground laughing, in an epileptic fit!"

"My ears are as wide open as canyons."

"Saturday morning, I was feeling ill, but I mean completely ill: *broken down*, as the English say. I thought I was done for. Thinking that I had dozed off, the nurse chatted quietly with my brother-in-law, about the municipal elections. One sentence struck me: 'Dr. Lehuppé,' she said, 'could very well win. He's quite popular around here.' A flash of genius suddenly struck me. A doctor candidate! That's the man for me. If I ask him to cure me so I could vote for him tomorrow, I might get better results: 'Bring me Dr. Lehuppé!' I cried in the feeble tones of the moribund. The good doctor arrives, a bit annoyed at this distraction from his electoral preoccupations. I give him my little pitch. 'I control,' I tell him, 'about thirty votes in this district, and so on and so forth.' So, there you have a man who auscultates me, palpates me, examines me every which way! He writes his prescription: 'Have someone fetch these remedies from the pharmacist... Or better yet, I'll go myself and bring them back for you.' A spoonful of medicine that he makes me swallow, which was, incidentally, rather disgusting; a liniment that he himself rubs in, etc., etc. He returns that evening, massages me again, gives me a pill, etc., etc. In short, I sleep as I have never slept in my life. And Sunday morning, back on my feet, old man, cured as if by magic!"

"Did you vote for him, at least?"

"Are you mad? An old conservative like me vote for some filthy progressive?"

FULL

As you see me now, my dear friends, I have not always rolled in millions of gold coins. My stables did not overflow with those thoroughbreds which are the glory of English breeding — in fact, I had no stables.

My garages — in fact, I had no garages — were bereft (oh, how lamentably!) of cherry-colored coupés and buttercup landaus, the honor of French manufacture.

At times — believe it or not — my immediate finances forbade the utilization of even a banal fiacre or vulgar taxi.

And when business or pleasure compelled me to mobilize my human body, my only resource remained the omnibus, and even — sadly, sometimes — the exclusive use of the double-decker.

One day (I was at that time a drummer with the Plège Circus — oh, my youth! — then in Versailles), I disembarked at the Saint-Lazare station, and headed for the Panthéon, to see a little girlfriend of mine, not very pretty, but so indulgent!

The buses arrived at the Madeleine in a state of truly indecent plenitude, especially the double-deckers.

And how hot it was!

The asphalt on the boulevards was like simmering licorice, and pedestrians' heels sank into it without a sound.

I don't quite recall why I refused to find a seat inside.

The excessive thermometrics that day, or the low ebb of my finances? No matter!

The buses arrived full from the place de Courcelles, and returned to the Panthéon even more full.

Therefore, I devised a stratagem devoid of scruples, but rather ingenious...

It was so long ago, my dear friends, that I can now recount my nasty little prank.

A bus on the Courcelles-Panthéon line dawned (like the sun) on the horizon.

I will add that it alone was as full as all of the preceding ones combined.

On a bit of a bench on the upper deck (a bitty bit of a bench, as we wisely used to say), sat a ruddy fat gentleman of peevish appearance.

Nobody got off, and the vehicle continued on its way, slowly, because of the traffic.

I addressed the ruddy gentleman in terms from which I omitted all courtesy.

Notably, I reproached him for taking money from an old Englishwoman afflicted with alcoholism and morphinomania.

I added tumultuously that he had performed abortions upon his own grandmother which had caused the poor woman's death.

At first, the ruddy gentleman refused to believe that these undeserved accusations were directed at him.

He looked at his neighbors; his neighbors looked at him; and, at that point, there could be no mistake.

They were for him.

He raised his arm, brandished his cane, and cried, "Damn kid!"

I persisted.

Fortunately for you, my feminine readers, I am too well-bred to repeat here the insults of every description that I showered upon the ruddy gentleman.

The entire upper deck expressed unalloyed delight, but he became more and more irritated.

His coloring had gradually climbed the degrees separating brick red from vivid scarlet.

He continued to cry, "Damn kid!"; but still did not get off.

"What is it, then," I asked myself, "the supreme insult that will make him leave his bitty bit of bench?"

At that moment, I noticed that he was decorated with a military medal. An inspiration!

With uncommon vehemence, I accused him of writing to Herr von Caprivi a daily correspondence bristling with indiscretions about our military establishment.

I was not mistaken.

The vivid scarlet left the old soldier's face, and he blanched livid with rage.

He left the bus.

I, by a quick turning motion, rushed from the right side to the left, passing in front of the horses, and while the ruddy gentleman sought his unknown blasphemer, I settled comfortably into his seat, on the bitty bit, etc.

The ruddy gentleman didn't find me, but since a foppish fool was laughing uproariously at the incident, he gave him a Homeric beating.

And I had no pity for the foppish fool, for one must never laugh at the misfortunes of others.

A HALLUCINATION

EXPLAINED AS EASILY AS POSSIBLE

The Easter holiday was favored with exceptional weather. On Sunday and Monday, numerous Parisians took advantage of it to travel, with their families, into the country.

The amount of ham and cold veal that they consumed, on the grass, was practically prodigious.

The *Journal*'s record keepers, assigned specially to this statistic, report a truly extraordinary result: 740,000 tons! A number which, we believe, has not been equalled since the summer of 1879.

The summer of 1879, we hasten to add, will remain legendary in the annals of the consumption of ham and cold veal.

On this occasion, let us thank our excellent colleague Baïssass, who, quite obligingly, took upon himself the role of record keeper, and brought surprising energy and perfect tact to the task.

As for me, I profited from the holiday by making my annual pilgrimage to the gingerbread fair, in the company of two excellent comrades, who were none other than Monseigneur the Duke of Aumale and M. Gidel, the amiable headmaster of the Condorcet school.

We had soon had enough, my friends and I, of the intolerable dust that suffuses the avenues of Vincennes, and, quite thirsty, installed ourselves on the terrace of a brasserie on the place du Trône, where we were served three mugs of a little *pissen-brau*, and I need say no more.

We chatted of one thing and another. The Duke of Aumale teems with piquant reminiscences, and Gidel literally scintillates with ingenious observations.

In short, we conversed with all our might.

Before us stood a booth, not yet open, with a sign in Russian letters.

An enormous picture, on the front, showed a tall Slavic woman who seemed to be on friendly terms with a sort of tzar dressed all in white.

What did they sell in that booth? I never learned, but it was a handsome booth, solidly constructed, and rich in appearance.

A line of dots, by way of abridgment.

.....

Suddenly, right in the middle of a rather risqué story from Gidel, I saw Henri... (I refer to the Duke of Aumale. Heavens! It's not as if we just met yesterday!)

I saw Henri, I say, whose face had become white, and whose eyes were opened wide in astonishment.

"What?" I asked, worried. "What's the matter?"

And Henri, pale, his arm extended, stammered:

"The Russian booth! The Russian booth!"

The color drained from our faces as well.

The Russian booth was no longer there!

The Russian booth that we had been admiring only five minutes ago, the Russian booth was no longer there!

It was too much!

They had not had time to move it. And besides, we would have noticed.

Henri, Gidel, and I racked our brains to the bursting point.

There was a minute of inexpressible anguish.

Suddenly, Gidel burst into that laughter so familiar to the students at Condorcet:

"My God," he cried, "how stupid we are!"

"???"

"The Russian booth..."

"Yes, the Russian booth?"

"Well, the Russian booth is still there."

"???"

"We're the ones who changed cafe."

A NEW KIND OF ILLUMINATION

"Well, if it isn't old Lafoucade! How are you?"

"Never better."

"And what are you doing in Paris?"

"I came here in the hope of raising some capital to start a promising business."

"Oh, bah! What kind of business?"

"An idea that came to me a few years ago in Tonkin. One evening, our spies informed us that a band of pirates had taken refuge in a village a few kilometers away. Quickly, we form a column, with Lieutenant Cornuel in command, and off we go. A black night, my friend, and I mean black! You would have thought yourself in a coal mine in Taupin. No moon, no stars in the sky, and no streetlights in the rice paddies!"

"You don't say!"

"Suddenly, we find ourselves illuminated, on both sides, by a light that is soft, strange, and fantastic. We seemed to be walking in golden gaslight. We look around, and see... Can you guess?"

"Don't keep me in suspense!"

"Tigers, old man! A pack of tigers. The eyes of the animals shone like embers, and their combined gaze produced a superb light."

"Wonderful!"

"Since that time, I've been tormented by the idea of putting that splendid illumination into practice. I've been working on the matter, and will soon launch the *Society for Illumination by the Eyes of Tigers*. To begin with, it will be more picturesque than gas or electricity. Upon elegant cast iron columns, we'll install cages containing adult tigers. Strong cages, of course, since a *tiger leak* would be a more dangerous inconvenience than a gas leak."

"Oh! You would notice it immediately."

"Probably. When you felt sharp fangs indiscreetly penetrating your thigh, you would say: Well, there must be a *tiger leak* around here."

"Gasmen would be replaced by trainers: it would be much more entertaining."

"It would be charming, I tell you!"

"But don't you think that the initial investment..."

"Not as much as you think, because the *Society for Illumination by the Eyes of Tigers* would do like the *Gas Company*, and realize enormous profits from the byproducts. Did you know, for example, that tiger dung is excellent for rhododendrons and petunias?"

"A good idea, that."

"There's no time to lose in developing the business. I'll send you a prospectus. Goodbye, old man."

"One of these days, Lafoucade."

.....

I had the opportunity, a few days ago, to meet the aforementioned Cornuel (an excellent fellow).

"Tell me," I said, a bit warily, "did you meet many tigers in Tonkin?"

"Not a one! The only tiger I saw in Indochina was an old one in the Saigon zoo, a poor old blind tiger that looked more like a bathmat than a dangerous carnivore."

CRUEL ENIGMA

Then what?...
Raoul Ponchon

Parisian life swarms with mysteries, large and small, often inexplicable, whose heroes carry their secrets into the grave.

Many Parisians, and some of the best, are prematurely bald from constantly tearing out their hair, seeking the key to the enigma. Cruel enigma!

I have heard, I who speak to you now, many mysterious stories which can be explained only by black magic, astral projection, or demonic influence.

One, among others:

I will not introduce you to M. Flanchard, an insignificant cuckold, devoid of interest.

Another kettle of fish entirely, Mme. Flanchard. Simply exquisite.

Quite temperamentuous, Mme. Flanchard had long ago contracted the habit of lightening the heavy chains of hymen by the pink buoys of adultery. (I assume, of course, that life is an ocean.)

At the time that our story begins, she had as a friend a pretty little man, no bigger than that, but strong despite his size, and as nice as you please. Are not the best ointments found in the smallest pots? Is not a little glass of fine burgundy, I ask you, better than the most capacious goblet filled to overflowing?

Mme. Flanchard adored her little lover, and told him so in no uncertain terms.

And it seemed to her — women are so funny! — that her sin was less cardinal with such a slight accomplice, and, besides, less ostentatious than with a drum major in the Republican Guard, especially one in full uniform.

Upon this last point, Mme. Flanchard showed sound common sense.

Upon the first, she was dead wrong. The dimensions of lovers have nothing to do with the offense. Wives should know this!

A married woman who sleeps with Edouard Philippe is just as guilty as another who consents to adulterous relations with Pascalis.

Let us close this parenthesis, because of the draft, and return to our muttons.

Mme. Flanchard lived in the suburb of Saint-Germain, and her miniature lover on the rue des Martyrs (almost across from me).

The woman often went in search of her beloved. The two miscreants then boarded a coach and went off wherever they pleased (which is none of our business).

Well, one day last week — as you can see, this is not medieval history—Mme. Flanchard and her friend took a coach on Urbaine — to be precise — and ordered the driver to take them to the corner of rue des Martyrs and faubourg Montmartre. After that, they would see.

The conversation soon became tender, ardent, insistent.

"No, Alfred," the lady said gently, "not here, there are too many people in the street."

"What difference does that make?" insisted Alfred. "We don't care what people think!"

"In a little while."

"No, now."

This last word was spoken with such authority that Mme. Flanchard could no longer resist the proposition — of what? I haven't a clue — from her little man.

And here the mystery begins.

The intersection of the rues de Maubeuge, Châteaudun, and

faubourg Montmartre is one of the deadliest crossroads in Paris.

Pedestrians, taxis, buses, and funerals all seem to meet there. There are, at any moment, nameless bottlenecks, and it is not uncommon to witness the joyful eradication of someone on foot.

(The day before yesterday, my coupé ran over an elderly woman, and it gave me a rather uncomfortable jolt.)

The fiacre that was transporting Mme. Flanchard's love life had to do like the others, and get in line, at a crawl.

Just then, on the sidewalk, appeared M. Flanchard.

Try to explain this phenomenon, O gross materialists: Suddenly, M. Flanchard felt within his breast the terrible shock of premonition.

With the unconscious assurance of a somnambulist, he walked straight ahead, without a second's hesitation, to the guilty hackney.

He was not mistaken: his wife was there, but SHE WAS THERE ALONE.

Nobody, you understand, had left the car, and yet *she was there alone!*

Delighted at his error, Flanchard withdrew, radiant that he had such a faithful spouse.

This mysterious business now becomes more complicated. A few minutes later, THERE WERE TWO in the fiacre.

Nobody, you understand, had entered the car, and yet *there were two!*

There were even two who seemed to be having a wonderful time.

Blushing, Mme. Flanchard admitted her anxiety at the encounter.

And, in a tone of gently scolding triumph, the little man said:

"You see. eh?... And you didn't want to!"

.....

Parisian life swarms with mysteries, large and small, often inextricable, whose heroes carry their secrets into the grave.

AN IMPORTANT REFORM IN THE WESTERN RAILWAY COMPANY

Let us recall the facts succinctly.

A few months ago, a certain Perrin (Emile) precipitously descended the stairs of a building on the rue Saint-Lazare, crying, "My wife has been murdered!"

The concierge and several other people rushed up to the designated apartment, which they found in great disorder.

The dresser drawers, the closet door, everything was open, including the throat of the tenant, a lady of the evening named Louise Lamier.

The police immediately suspected a crime.

The inquiry revealed that the aforementioned Perrin, an employee of the Western Railway Company, lived maritally — meritoriously, some wags put it — with the victim. His accounts of the latter's earnings were kept with a care and punctuality rarely encountered in the books of the largest companies.

Out of jealousy, probably, the big cheeses of the Saint-Lazare station lost no time in sending M. Perrin back to his private studies.

I was outraged at this brutal dismissal of a model employee, and went to ask around the offices of the Western Company, to see how they justified it.

In the absence of the General Secretary, I was cordially received by M. Charles Raymond.

"My God," he said, "the thing couldn't be simpler. The public may not know this, but the Western Railway Company has always attached great importance to its employees' feminine connections. We don't ask, of course, that they bankrupt themselves for the ladies, but under no pretext will we tolerate them shacking up with one of those creatures who lives by her charms. After the affair at rue Saint-Lazare, new regulations were enacted on the subject.

"Here's the gist of it: under 2,400 francs a year, unmarried employees may only consort with women in small businesses: fruiterers, dairywomen, tinkers' wives. The gradation continues. The more an employee makes, the higher he may aim his affections. So it is that the most important functionaries in our administration have mistresses in banking, commerce, the judiciary..."

"The clergy?"

"Comedian! As for the directors, they will be summarily dismissed if they have even one little girlfriend who is not a princess from one of the current or former reigning families of Europe."

"All the same, you were certainly harsh with your poor Perrin! Instead of brutally firing him, couldn't you have found a position suited to his talents: at the harbor station in Dieppe, for example, or, even better, with one of the shuttles serving the fish trade?"

"We considered it, but those gentlemen preferred to make an example of him."

"And Dreux, the other employee implicated in this regrettable affair?"

"Dreux will be kept in his current position. He is, after all, a model employee, good-natured, affable, and easier to talk to than his often disagreeable superiors. Hence the axiom familiar in the Western Railway Company: *Trust in God, but keep your partner Dreux* (the word *God* here used in the sense of *boss*)."

The interview had come to an end. I thanked M. Raymond, and we parted after a glass of white wine at the Terminus.

LIKE A FISH

One afternoon, as we strolled along the avenue de l'Opéra, the young woman on my arm said:

"I wouldn't mind a snack."

And we entered a fashionable patisserie.

While my companion ate and drank a thousand alimentary frivolities, I, having no appetite — the sordid orgy of the night before, probably — I contemplated the sporadic ambiance.

Two young women entered, like acolytes.

One well-to-do, the other humble.

The other — obviously! — the teacher of the one.

And they sat down.

Both pretty, but differently.

The teacher, blonde and slender, but too slender — desiccated, perhaps — and blonde, but a poor blonde, it seemed, washed out by poverty and humiliation.

Slender also, the young student, and blonde. But what finesse, and what blondness!

As fine as amber gathered in some improbable Baltic land, and as blonde as the purest gold melted in those crucibles most famed for the refinement of pure gold.

Very sweet, however, and with perfect manners, the young student was gracious and courteous to her teacher, for which I thanked her, deep in the cajolery of my heart.

And this is what I saw:

One of the patisserie waitresses, without waiting for an order — they were obviously regulars — brought two plates, two glasses of madeira, babas au rhum, and biscuits.

The instructor nibbled meekly on a biscuit.

The wealthy young woman delicately grasped, between her gloved fingers, a glass of madeira, and...

I would say: *she drank it,* but that would scarcely convey the action that was accomplished.

A suction pump, powered by a 120 horsepower motor, could not have emptied that glass more rapidly or more formally.

I have seen, in my life, many people drink like fish; I have seen the draining of many glasses, bottles, and even liters. I have witnessed an infinite number of bibulous exploits, but never, never in my life, has a cup, before my eyes, been more rapidly emptied.

The young woman continued her lunch with the babas au rhum.

Her instructor kept nibbling on the biscuits.

When the babas au rhum were finished, the young woman seized the teacher's madeira, and... hup!

The same performance as above.

"Bravo!" I thought to myself. "You're in fine form, my little one!"

The little one called, in a pretty, softly modulated voice, "Miss?"

The waitress who had already served them ran over.

With a little circular gesture, the young woman indicated that the refreshments, both liquid and solid, should be replenished.

Biscuits and babas au rhum were brought, and two fresh madeiras were poured.

The babas au rhum and the two madeiras soon followed the same path — and what a path! — as their precursors.

Without using an abacus,[1] I undertook this calculation — simple, but perfectly capable of troubling my impassivity:

Here was a young lady of seventeen years, who, in less than five minutes, had introduced six babas au rhum and four glasses of madeira into her economy.

Without bothering to find the age of the captain, I concluded that she was a hot-blooded number.

With rather malicious curiosity, I waited for the moment when this intrepid madeira-emptier would stumble to her feet.

But I did not get my money's worth.

She arose, as might arise any young woman who had just drunk a glass of watered wine, and walked out to the street, calm, fresh, smiling, and followed by her humble instructor.

In the following days, I often thought about that little scene, and the desire overtook me to witness it again.

I reconstituted the details.

A Tuesday, five o'clock, a music folder: a singing lesson, probably, or piano.

And the next Tuesday, a little before five, I reinstalled myself in the patisserie.

Not in vain was my wait.

Soon, they entered.

Once again, the teacher nibbled the biscuits.

The young woman made her four madeiras and six babas au rhum vanish, as if by enchantment.

I followed them.

Well, fancy that, I was not mistaken.

They entered a building which bore, on the corner of the gate, a vast copper plaque: *Music Lessons, Piano, Solfeggio, etc.*

The lesson will last an hour, I thought; and I took a place on the terrace of a nearby cafe, which offered me a vantage point which was *jolly convenient*, as the English say.

At the stroke of six, the young women emerged.

They went up the avenue de l'Opéra, and reached, by the most direct route, the boulevard Malesherbes.

An immense American patisserie, quite popular at the time (do you remember?) lay in that neighborhood.

Without hesitation, as if by routine, they entered.

It was then the same scene as on the avenue de l'Opéra, with slight variations: the madeira replaced by port, the size of the glasses doubled, and the young miss, finding the babas too dry, insisted that they be moistened with a copious affusion of rum, and specified that the rum be of the brand (*space for rent*).

She paid, arose, and departed, without anything in her graceful walk betraying the generous amount of wine stored in her little belly, not to mention the additional rum.

I would have enjoyed recontemplating this spectacle, but, around this time, my cover was blown in Paris, and I had to go look for suckers in the unexplored provinces.

No sooner had I returned to Paris, when I received a wedding announcement. My friend Léon Delarue, the well-known electrician, was marrying Mademoiselle Jane A..., and invited me to the nuptial benediction and the ball.

At the altar, I recognized the bride.

You too, clever readers, will recognize her: she was the formidable gourmandizer of the avenue de l'Opéra and the boulevard Malesherbes.

And how pretty she was in white!

At the ball, she was exquisiteness itself.

Everyone envied my friend Delarue.

The bride's eyes shone like rubies.

Their color would have made the most imperial cherries of Montmorency seem livid, and I knew, myself, that their crimson was not exclusively due to modesty.

The couple, at a given moment, disappeared, furtive.

Dujardin's verses from *The Knight of the Past* buzzed in my temples:

And she will give herself, nonverbally,
To all his dangerous hyperbole.

And — foolishly — on the way home, I felt all funny.

---

1. The abacus is an instrument used for calculation, by means of beads on strings. The Chinese use it regularly, and call it *suanpan*.

THE FALSE BLASPHEMER

The rain had surprised me at the beginning of the rue de Rennes, across from the burlesque statue of the late lamented Diderot.

A sad, gray, obstinate downpour.

If I were to tell you that I'd forgotten my umbrella, I would be lying: No umbrella have I got. (On sunny days I'm set, when it starts to rain I'm not, and then I get all wet, as the song says.)

What to do? Seek refuge in a coach gate? That is not my privilege.

Go into a cafe and wait for the rain to stop? I have never set foot in a cafe and will not begin at my age.

The church of Saint-Germain-des-Prés offered its porch. I literally rushed to it.

From up in heaven, his final residence, the late Germain des Prés must have been delighted, for his holy place was as crowded as in the most glorious times of the Christian faith.

Old ladies especially, and young women, and children. And men too.

Some women, probably of a practical turn of mind, were determined not to waste their time. They could be seen using their enforced stay in the church for prayers and signs of the cross, as they might have done their knitting, had the situation called for it.

And the rain still fell.

A gray light filtered through the violet windows, suffusing the air with a vague, hovering unease.

Outside, streetcars passed, and their horns blared a raucous clamor, like death.

The little chandeliers eternally alight before the tabernacle blinked, like sad tired eyes.

I was close to the altar of the Virgin.

And I saw something strange.

By the side door of the Boulevard Saint-Germain, a little old woman entered, filthy, frighteningly wrinkled, an abject pauper to whom I gave a few coins, out of fear.

Her rags were thoroughly soaked.

Tottering, she headed down the aisle to the Virgin.

About fifteen meters from the altar, she stopped short and stood erect.

At the base, in gold on blue, shone, around the Queen of the Angels, the inscription: *Consolatrix afflictorum.*

The beggar sketched a hasty sign of the cross, and stayed there, her hands in her old camisole, hunched over.

Somewhat astonished to find religious sentiments in such a miserable old woman, I could not take my eyes from her.

At first, she seemed to be imploring.

And then, little by little, her attitude changed.

She straightened, as well as she could, her feeble frame. Her arms were crossed high across her chest, and she seemed, the unhappy woman, to be defying the mother of our Lord.

In the interest of veracity, I should add that Saint Joseph's wife seemed to take no notice of this impertinence.

The rain stopped; the church emptied.

There was nobody near the Virgin except two or three worshippers, the pauper, and me.

And then I understood.

Poor old woman! She was standing on a heating grate.

She wasn't blaspheming: she was drying.

HALF AND HALF

Pantodramedy in eleven tableaus, for the Theater of the
National Institute for Blind Children

ARGUMENT

FIRST TABLEAU

The stage shows the terrace of a brasserie with British preten-sions. On the window, the tardy pedestrian (it is a quarter to noon) can read: American Drinks, Luncheon, Pale Ale, Stout.

Unwittingly, it evokes two lines by the poet Alphonse Allais:

Stout, cider, sherry, tokay:
Sit outside or share it, okay?

SECOND TABLEAU

A pretty young woman takes a seat on the terrace, and raps on the zinc table with the end of her umbrella. Pierrot, the waiter, arrives.

THIRD TABLEAU

Pierrot, stricken to the marrow by the young woman's charms, asks what she will *have*.

The young woman expresses a desire for a vermouth-cassis, but please, not too much cassis.

FOURTH TABLEAU

As soon as Pierrot goes back into the establishment, to procure the necessary ingredients for a vermouth-cassis, two obvious snobs take their place at a table, not far from the exquisite creature.

FIFTH TABLEAU

Pierrot returns. He serves the adored one, not without some trouble, and inquires of the ridiculous nonentities what they will *have*.

The imbeciles in question order a pint of *half and half*, which is a mixture of pale ale and stout, as black as Erebus.

SIXTH TABLEAU

Troubled, more than words can tell, by the presence of the lovely young woman, Pierrot makes a mistake, and, instead of a pint of *half and half*, brings a pint of ale.

SEVENTH TABLEAU

The snobs squeal, much like stuck pigs.

EIGHTH TABLEAU

Pierrot, extremely embarrassed by his error, for the owner has a fiery temper, goes back inside with the beer, and starts to set things aright when...

NINTH TABLEAU

...He has a clever idea. He takes the establishment's inkstand, pours a few drops of ink into the ale, and, with a winning smile, takes the unusual mixture back to them.

TENTH TABLEAU

The snobs drink it, and find it good.

ELEVENTH TABLEAU

So good, that when they depart, they leave Pierrot a hefty tip, with which he supports the pretty young woman.

ESSAY
ON A NEW DIVISION OF FRANCE

I have just put the finishing touches on a little work with which — shall I admit it? — I am extremely satisfied.

My first step was to show it to my friend Captain Cap, former starter at the Ottawa Observatory (the same whom I mentioned recently, who scheduled the departures of shooting stars).

With all the graciousness in the world, Captain Cap professed that, since Strabo, no geographical conception comparable to mine had seen the light of day.

"Galileo himself, who was no nitwit," added Cap, "would not have thought of it."

This little flattering preamble in place, let us proceed to the crux of the matter:

You have certainly noticed that we give the name "Midi"—that is, "Noon"—to the meridional section of France.

I go to the Noon. I come from the Noon.

His doctors advised him to spend winter in the Noon. He has a Noon accent, etc., etc. These are common expressions that we hear every day, and which none of us, I wager, ever thinks of protesting, so natural have they become.

But why?

Why does the south alone benefit from this chronometric designation, while no other part of France is called *Midnight* or *A quarter to four*?

I repeat, this state of affairs does not answer to the ideals of justice that we cherish in our hearts; and I believe that I have originated a little plan that will eliminate such flagrant partiality.

There would be no more complaints, and France would remain France, whereas the French people would not cease being French for an instant.

Here is my plan. (I give it to you for what it's worth, although I consider it not much stupider than many ideas set forth by members of the Institute.)

We would divide France (figuratively, of course, since it's already divided enough as it is, the poor dear) into twelve latitudinal slices, each named after an hour of the clock.

The *Noon* would still be the *Noon*; the slice above it would be called *Eleven o'clock*, the one above that *Ten o'clock*, and so on, moving north.

The slice containing Dunkirk would consequently be called *One o'clock*.

All of this may strike you as somewhat bizarre, since you're unfamiliar with it; but the first time someone said, "I'm from the Noon," it also seemed funny, you may be sure.

And then, while we're at it, nothing prevents us from dividing France vertically, as we have just divided it horizontally, that is to say, along the longitudes.

We would create seven zones, each named after a day of the week, beginning with the area around Brest, which we would call *Monday*, and ending with the eastern border, over there (let us always think it, but never say it) which would be called *Sunday*.

We establish in this way ever so many little squares, whose names alone indicate their positions precisely, much more clearly than with the foolish and outmoded system of longitudes and latitudes.

Paris, for example, if I am not mistaken, would be found at *Thursday-five o'clock*.

My plan, as you can see, is a simple one; too simple, in fact, to be adopted by the gentlemen of the government.

I can imagine the face of the director of the Bureau of Longitudes.

Have you ever, in Barcelona, seen a big cheese shrug his shoulders?

THE GOOD-NATURED MANAGER

WHO WAS A LITTLE SARCASTIC, AND THE EMPLOYEE WHO WAS COMPLETELY IRRESPONSIBLE

A SCOTTISH STORY

Lucy, my pretty little British girlfriend, my oh so blond, as the poets say, told me a story that filled me with joy.

It happened, apparently, in Scotland. But no importance should be given to that detail, for it could just as well have happened in Hanover, Rouergue, the Palatinate, or the Auge Valley.

The story will be improved by being read, in places, with a slight English accent:

Young Alexander MacAstrol was a charming lad, gifted with a friendly face and with irrepressible cheerfulness.

A consummate musician, well versed in the thousand temptations of his age and sex, he also excelled in all sports and games, which made him popular with the best families of Edinboro (the customary national way to pronounce and spell *Edinburgh*).

Unfortunately, these sterling qualities were spoiled by the atrocious defect of laziness. Alexander MacAstrol was as lazy as all of the dormice in creation, including the painter Luigi "Dormouse" Loir himself.

In addition, he was irresponsible in business: when sent on urgent errands, he lingered for hours smoking cigarettes on Prince Street, as the French do on their grand boulevards.

And when the manager entered Alexander's office unexpectedly, he often found Alexander practicing the sword dance — with the claymores replaced by umbrellas.

What a good boss, the manager of the *Central Pneumatic Bank (Limited)*!

Never, on his part, one word louder than another! Never a gesture of impatience!

When an employee was remiss in his duties, Mr. MacRyno-linn — for that was his name — called him into his office, joked a bit, sometimes perpetrated a pun on his name, and then sent him on his way.

.....

A few days later—the date is unimportant — young Alexander MacAstrol put on his most tearful face to announce to Mr. Mac-Rynolinn that one of his aunts — one of MacAstrol's — had just died, and that he would be grateful to have the next day off, to attend the dear old lady's funeral.

"But, of course!" acquiesced the excellent Mr. MacRynolinn. "That's only proper!... Have fun, my friend."

The following day, the manager of the *Central Pneumatic Bank (Limited)* was taking a walk with several French friends.

Among these Frenchmen was a certain Taupin, whom it amused Mr. MacRinolynn enormously to call Sir Blackburn, nobody knew why.

...with several French friends, as I was saying, when he saw, fishing in the Codfly—a small river that lets into the Forth — a young man who furiously resembled Alexander MacAstrol.

So furiously, in fact, that it was Alexander MacAstrol himself.

The genial manager chose not to bother his assistant during an activity that he seemed to enjoy so.

But, the next morning, young Alexander learned from a page that the manager expected him in his office.

"Ah, there you are, my friend!" said Mr. MacRinolynn. "Have a seat... or rather, don't have a seat, for I'll be brief."

Alexander did not have a seat and the manager continued, toying with his whiskers:

"The next time that you have the misfortune to lose your aunt, please have the kindness to bring me a few fillets."

REVERSIBILITY

"My poor friend, I don't mean this as a reproach," I told him, "but you look like a man who is exhausted."

(Those were not my exact words; I believe I even told him that he *looked like crap*... But I have resolved to bring to my writings far more decorum than is shown in my daily life.)

The man thus addressed gave me a long and melancholy look, shook my hand with a limp grip, and let out a sigh as deep as a tomb.

At that moment, a lady and gentleman passed, who greeted my friend and exchanged a few words with him.

While they chat, I will take the opportunity to introduce the gentleman with the debilitated appearance.

Bearer of one of the greatest names in French heraldry, heir to a patrimony with which you or I would be quite content, a handsome man and a nice fellow, my old comrade, the young Duke Honneau de la Lunerie possessed all of the privileges of perfect felicity. Unfortunately, a penchant for occultism, extreme credulity, and a foolish trust in others disarmed him for the rough battle of life, and got him into countless jams. You could have sold that lad London Bridge, and he would have tipped you.

He regularly socialized with that phony magus, the Big Cheese of Limburger, the Sâr Jynt at Arms, with no offense to that ogival and gymnopedic musician named Erik Satie, whom I recently baptized (how clever I am) Esoterik Satie.[1]

Despite his many faults and my sly reserve, we got along quite well, the Duke Honneau and I.

I would even give him a hand when tables didn't tip quickly enough, and whisper ingenious insights, couched in a lapidary style, to the ghosts of history's greatest corpses.

Now that you know the young count as well as if you made him, let me take up the thread of my story.

"Ah, my poor friend!" he cried. "If you knew what has happened to me!"

"What afflicts you, O Duke?"

"Something rather unpleasant in itself, but whose extent surpasses everything recorded to date in the matter of materialization and psychic correspondence. Are you familiar with the experiments of Lieutenant Colonel Rochas?"

"I've heard of them."

On the impossible chance that one of my readers has never heard of the experiments conducted by Lieutenant Colonel Rochas d'Aiglun (Eugène Auguste Albert), officer of the Legion of Honor, I shall succinctly summarize them.

This senior officer of genius, director of the Polytechnic Institute, raised in the severe school of *2 plus 2 is 4*, neither a crackpot nor a hoaxer, is currently performing for us a little series of operations which, in the middle ages, would have sufficed for the combustion of a thousand and some sorcerers.

He models a little wax statuette in your image, *exteriorizes* your senses, and transfers them into his little work of art.

And there you are enchanted!

A pinprick on the statue's forehead, and you feel a sharp pain on your own forehead.

Hold a lit match to the statuette's arm, and you suffer a burn on your own arm.

Put booties that are a bit too tight on the statuette's feet, and you discover that you have corns, on your own feet.

Not only disagreeable sensations are transmitted. Others too.

For example...

But I stop, for not all of my readers have, like Lieutenant Colonel Rochas, developed brows that can no longer blush.

Duke Honneau, naturally, had followed, with the greatest interest, the old soldier's curious experiments.

"But what I would never have believed," he told me, "is that one could obtain, in this kind of phenomenon, such a fantastic case of reversibility."

"Explain yourself."

"Do you insist?... It just hurts me so."

"Go on, I'll console you."

"Very well, here it is... You know that I have long been deeply in love with Félicienne de Domfront. What misunderstandings have prevented me from obtaining her favors? I still don't know. Life in Paris is filled with such mysteries: here is a pretty girl I desire, who surely doesn't find me repellant, for whom I would make the greatest sacrifices, and then... nothing! Well, one day I had the idea of trying out Rochas's experiment on her and me. I had a statuette made of Félicienne. I transferred into it, unbeknownst to her, her senses. The results were conclusive. Even when she was far away, I remained in communication with her. At certain regular times, I kissed the statuette, on the forehead, for example, and Félicienne, at that moment, felt an agreeable sensation on her own forehead. My friends, trusted friends, whom I had assigned to the control, affirmed the fact on several occasions. But the most curious, and at the same time most painful result, was the case of reversibility that I mentioned."

"I don't understand."

"But you do understand! Don't ask me for a precise and depressing explanation."

The truth was, I was mystified.

I didn't grasp the full horror of the situation until a few minutes later, when, in a brasserie on the boulevard, I ordered an excellent glass of beer, and he had nothing but weak orgeat.

P. S.: To spare the reader useless anxiety, I will add this: My friend, Duke Honneau, did not limit himself, in those experiments, to simple psychic communications. Perhaps physical contact is not unknown to this strange phenomenon. Back to you, Lieutenant Colonel Rochas. A. A.

---

1. I sincerely hope that my good friend Erik Satie finds no hint of acrimony in these remarks. And if he does, he knows where to find me. (I am much stronger than he.) A. A.

THE TEMPLARS

There was a man for you, a rugged man, and full of fire! Twenty times have I seen him bring the whole company to a halt, simply by squeezing his horse between his thighs.

He was a brigadier then. A bit rough in the camp, but charming in town.

What the devil was his name? Some damn Alsatian name that I can't remember, like Wurtz or Schwartz... Yes, that must be it, Schwartz. Besides, his name isn't important. From Neufbrisach, not Neufbrisach itself, but the area.

What a man, that Schwartz!

One Sunday morning (we were stationed in Oran), Schwartz said to me, "What shall we do today?" And I answered, "Whatever you like, Schwartz, old man."

So, we agreed to go sailing.

We take a boat, *row, boys, row!*, and there we are out at sea.

It was a beautiful day, a bit of wind, but beautiful all the same.

We sped like an arrow, happy to see the coast of Africa disappear on the horizon.

Rowing works up an appetite! Good Lord, what a lunch!

I especially remember a knuckle of ham which we devoured almost indecently.

During this time, we failed to notice that the wind had turned colder, and that the waves were becoming disconcertingly choppy.

"Oh, hell!" said Schwartz. "We'd better..."

In fact, no, Schwartz wasn't his name.

He had a longer name, something like Schwartzbach. Schwartzbach it is!

Well then, Schwartzbach said to me, "Kid, we'd better think of rallying."

Rallying, in a pig's eye. The wind blew up into a storm.

The sail is blown away by a squall, an oar takes off, swept away by a wave. There we are at the mercy of the elements.

We were swept into the open sea, with deplorable speed and horrific turbulence.

Ready for anything, we stripped off our boots and jackets.

Night fell, the hurricane raged.

Ah! What a fine idea that was, to go contemplate your azure, O Mediterranean!

Eventually, it became completely dark. It was close to midnight.

Suddenly, a frightening thump. We had reached land.

Where were we?

Schwartzbach, or rather Schwartzbacher, I remember now, it was Schwartzbacher, Schwartzbacher, I say, who knew his geography like the back of his hand (Alsatians are very knowledgeable), said to me:

"We're on the Isle of Rhodes, old man."

Strictly between us, shouldn't the government post signs identifying all the islands in the Mediterranean, since you have a devil of a time telling them apart, when you're not used to it?

It was as dark as the inside of an oven. As wet as soup, we clambered up the rocks of the cliff.

Not a light on the horizon. It was jolly.

"We'll miss roll call tomorrow morning," I said, just to say something.

"And tomorrow evening, too," Schwartzbacher glumly replied.

And we walked through sparse gorse and prickly broom. We walked without knowing where, simply to keep warm.

"Ah," cried Schwartzbacher, "I can make out a light over there, do you see it?"

I followed the direction of Schwartzbacher's finger, and there was in fact a light, but very far off, a strange kind of light.

And we kept walking, faster now.

Finally we arrived.

Upon the rocks arose a castle of imposing aspect, a high stone castle, which looked as if it wasn't much fun inside.

One of the castle towers served as a chapel, and the light that we had seen was the sacred illumination filtering through the tall gothic windows.

Chanting wafted to us, low male chanting, chanting that sent a shiver down your spine.

"Let's go in," said Schwartzbacher, firmly.

"How?"

"Ah! Well, let's look for an exit."

Schwartzbacher said, "Let's look for an exit," but he meant, "Let's look for an entrance." However, since it's the same thing, I thought it unnecessary to point out his error, which may have been nothing but a lapsus caused by the cold.

There were many entrances, but they were all locked, and there were no bells. So it was as if there were no entrances.

At last, after walking around the castle, we discovered a small wall that we could scale.

"Now," said Schwartzbacher, "let's look for the kitchen."

There may have been no kitchen in the building, for no odor of cooking came to tickle our nostrils.

We walked through an interminable maze of corridors.

Sometimes, a bat flew down, and brushed our faces with its filthy fur.

At the turn of a corridor, the chanting that we had heard struck our ears, coming from close by.

We were in a large room, that must have communicated with the chapel.

"I understand now," said Schwartzbacher (or rather Schwartzbachermann, I remember now), "we're in the castle of the Templars."

No sooner had he said those words, than an enormous iron door swung wide open.

We were flooded with light.

Men were there, on their knees, hundreds of them, armored in iron, helmets on their heads, and of giant stature.

They arose with a great clanking of iron, turned, and saw us.

With one accord, they cried, "Draw swords!", and marched toward us, blades held high.

I would rather have been somewhere else.

With perfect command, Schwartzbachermann rolled up his sleeves, stood in a gesture of defiance, and loudly cried:

"Ah, by the Lord above! Templars, if you were a hundred thousand, as sure as my name is Durand…"

Ah! I remember now, his name was Durand. His father was a tailor in Aubervilliers. Durand, yes, that's it…

Good old Durand! What a man!

THE STORY OF LITTLE STEPHEN GIRARD

AND OF ANOTHER LITTLE BOY WHO HAD READ THE STORY OF
LITTLE STEPHEN GIRARD

after Mark Twain

I

There exists in Philadelphia a man who—when he was just a poor little boy — entered a bank and said:

"Excuse me, sir, you wouldn't need a little boy?"

"No, little boy," answered the majestic banker, "I don't need a little boy."

His heart full, tears on his cheeks, sobs in his throat, the little boy descended the marble staircase, sucking a barley-sugar that he had bought with a sou stolen from his good and pious aunt.

Concealing his noble form, the banker hid behind a door, persuaded that the little boy was going to throw a stone at him.

The little boy, in fact, had picked up something from the ground: it was a pin, which he attached to his poor but shabby coat.

"Come here!" cried the banker to the little boy.

The little boy came here.

"What did you pick up?" asked the majestic banker.

"A pin," replied the little boy.

The financier continued:

"Are you good, little boy?"

The little boy said that he was good.

"How do you vote?... Oh, I'm sorry, do you go to Sunday school?"

The little boy said that he went.

Then, the banker dipped a golden pen into the purest of inks, wrote on a scrap of paper *St. Peter*, and asked the little boy what it meant.

The little boy replied that it meant *Salt Peter*.

"No," said the banker, "it means *Saint Peter*."

The little boy said "Oh!"

The banker took a liking to the little boy, and the little boy again said "Oh!"

Then, the banker brought the little boy into his business, and gave him half of the profits and all of the capital.

And later, the little boy married the banker's daughter.

Everything that the banker owned, it was the little boy who got it.

II

My uncle having told me the preceding story, I spent six weeks picking up pins from the ground, in front of a bank.

I was waiting for the banker to call out to me:

"Little boy, are you good?"

I would have answered that I was good.

He would have written *St. John*, and I would have said that it meant *Salt John*.

It's possible that the banker was in no hurry to have a partner, or that his daughter was a boy, for one day he called to me:

"Little boy, what are you picking up there?"

"Pins," I answered politely.

"Show them to me."

He took them, and I, I held my hat in my hand, ready to become his partner and to marry his daughter.

But that was not his invitation:

"Those pins," he roared, "belong to the bank; and if I find you sneaking around here again, I'll set the dog on you."

I left, leaving the old scoundrel in possession of my pins.

I must say, though: that's how it goes in real life!

POSTHUMOUS

Every evening, in those days, I went to a little cafe on the rue de Rennes, where I met a dozen of my comrades, all students and artists. Among the latter, a tall young fellow, a sculptor, very good-natured, even a bit naive. He was called, I never knew why, the *Refiner*.

One evening at the Tonnelier ball, the *Refiner* picked up a very pale young woman, whose big brown eyes sometimes shone with a curious gleam. He became quite attached to her, and, from then on, never left her.

Her name was Lucia.

We added *di Lammermoor*, which one wag in our circle changed to *Mère Moreau*. The name stuck.

Every evening, regularly, at nine o'clock, the *Refiner* and *Mère Moreau* arrived at the brasserie.

He played a game of billiards, while she sat behind the illustrated magazines, and gravely listened to our compliments on her beautiful black hair, her exquisite white skin, and her big brown eyes.

I don't recall how it began, but around that time we became obsessed with cards. *Poker* became our only god.

At our table, instead of the peaceful chats of yore, one heard: "Deal!..." "I raise you a hundred sous!..." "Two pairs for your king!..." "That doesn't beat a straight flush!"

One evening, the *Refiner* entered without Lucia.

"And *Mère Moreau*?" we asked in chorus.

"She's in Clamart, with one of her aunts who is quite ill."

The aunt in Clamart provoked, for all of us, a gentle smile.

That evening, the *Refiner* won every hand. We exchanged looks that clearly meant: Cuckold's luck!

But the *Refiner* was so amiable that we scrupulously avoided causing him any pain.

The next day, Lucia returned. With touching unanimity, we asked after the health of her aunt.

"A bit better, thank you. But she still needs a lot of care. I'll go back to see her Thursday."

On Thursday, in fact, the *Refiner* arrived alone. His luck from the other day returned, as insolent as before. It bothered him. He kept telling us:

"Really, my friends, it pains me to *rake in all of your bread* like this."

He would gladly have returned our *bread*.

The visits to the aunt in Clamart became more and more frequent, and always coincided with unbelievable luck for the *Refiner*.

So regularly, that eventually when we saw him arrive alone, nobody wanted to play.

He never suspected a thing. His faith in his Lucia was unshakable.

One evening, about midnight, he came in like a madman, pale, his hair on end.

"What's wrong?"

"Oh, if you only knew... Lucia..."

"Tell us!"

"She died... just now... in my arms."

We all arose and accompanied him back to his place.

It was true. Poor little *Mère Moreau* lay on the bed, her big brown eyes staring terribly.

She was buried the next day.

The *Refiner* was painful to see. As we left the cemetery, he begged us not to leave him.

We spent the evening together, trying to distract him.

When the brasserie closed, he was afraid of going home alone.

One of us took pity on him, and suggested:

"How about a little game of poker at my place?"

It was two in the morning. We began playing. All through the night, the *Refiner* won, as he had never won before, even in the palmiest days of the aunt in Clamart. Like a somnambulist, he collected his winnings, then loaned them back to us to continue the game.

His luck lasted until dawn, vertiginous, insane.

Without saying a word, we all had the same idea: This time, you couldn't say that Lucia was unfaithful.

The next day, we learned that she had been exhumed and violated during the night.

LÉON GANDILLOT

The physiognomy of Léon Gandillot—whose *Sub-Prefect of Château-Buzard* is now being performed with such success at the Palais-Royal—is too familiar to Parisians for me to attempt, once again, to describe him.

Physically, Gandillot is a small man, lean and high-strung, with a waxed mustache and an imperial. He is seldom without his monocle and riding crop.

Our acquaintance does not date from yesterday. We met in '48, during the days of June, at the time of the affair at the Arts-et-Métiers.

Gandillot was then secretary to Ledru-Rollin, and I the vice-consul of Venezuela in Amboise.

Both staunch republicans, personal friends of Arago and Garnier-Pagès, we never hesitated to shed our blood in defense of liberty.

Four years later, the coup d'état sent Gandillot to Lambessa, from which he was able to escape, disguised as a Maronite clergyman.

Gandillot reached Canada, where he created the clockwork brick industry, and from there went to the United States.

Léon Gandillot's immense fortune dates from this period.

It was he who had the idea of adapting the old world's methods of gallantry for the big cities of North America.

He rented vast apartment buildings, and brought from Europe in general, and the Saint-Georges neighborhood in particular, a number of lovely young women who were infinitely complacent and none too prudish.

Before six months had passed, he had established his clientele, and what a clientele!

All of Uncle Sam's best, in the way of clergymen, aldermen, and politicians.

A man of the world, a charming conversationalist, an indefatigable waltzer, a musician to his fingertips, Gandillot insisted that his houses be run perfectly: and he succeeded.

In 1866, we find Gandillot in Austria. At the battle of Koenigsgroetz — which we, in our ignorance of the German language, call the battle of Sadowa — Gandillot commanded the third Austrian corps, composed mostly of Tyrolians. These brave men, inspired by their leader's audacity, threw themselves, singing, onto the German lines. We all know the rest.

Then comes '70 and its somber aftermath. Gandillot returns to France, and strews the principal battlefields with his corpse.

We meet him in Froeshwiller, in Bazeilles, in Bourget, in Châteaudun, in Pont-Noyelles, in Patsy, in Dijon, etc.

We meet him everywhere.

His theatrical vocation only came later, and under conditions that are remarkable enough to be recounted here.

Greatly bothered by a case of blackmail, which we will have the good taste not to elucidate, M. Francisque Sarcey was desperately in need of money.

An archeologist in Montmartre, since deceased, known familiarly as Rabbit-Skin, introduced Francisque Sarcey and Léon Gandillot.

This last, taking pity on the sobbing critic, advanced him a sum which amounted, if memory serves, to almost thirty thousand francs, against which M. Sarcey gave him one hundred and some thousand francs in promissory notes.

Alas! The notes remained unpaid!

Gandillot was growing impatient, when M. Sarcey offered him a bargain:

"I have no money to give you," he said, "but I can pay you in publicity. Write some plays, and I'll say good things about them."

Throwing in the towel, Gandillot accepted.

He entered the first cafe that he saw, asked for pen and paper, and composed his *Clinging Women*.

The scheme worked wonderfully; and at the present time (3:20), M. Sarcey is nearly acquitted of his debt. One or two more plays, and M. Gandillot will no longer have to work in the theater.

Unless Gandillot, who spent considerable time with the black population of the United States, follows their example and keeps working.

P.S..: This morning, I received the following letter from M. Francisque Sarcey, which I hasten to reproduce:

Dear sir,

It is only at this moment that a column of yours has come to my attention, a column consecrated to Léon Gandillot, in which my name and character are irritatingly invoked.

I will not bother to correct the errors that teem throughout your biography, errors which have offended and seriously afflicted the friends of M. Gandillot. These corrections are not my business. Gandillot is big enough to come to his own defense.

What concerns me personally is an entirely different kettle of fish, and I insist, without delay, in offering a few explanations for the events that you mention in your column.

In urgent need of money, you say, quite bothered by an act of blackmail, I had to appeal to M. Gandillot's purse.

This is perfectly true. To avoid any misunderstanding, here is what happened:

It was a few days before Mademoiselle X... debuted at the Odéon. I had noticed the little one at the Conservatory competition, where she received a second prize in tragedy. I found her quite attractive, informed her of the fact, and expected that she would not debut at the Odéon without coming to say hello.

And so she did, or rather, did not, because the little rascal sent instead, guess who, her chambermaid.

I am extremely nearsighted. My word, I never suspected a thing. Besides, the soubrette, admirably directed, played her part to perfection.

She went so far as to recite some verses from a young neo-modern poet, whose name I've forgotten. I remember a few fragments. It was called "My Heart":

My heart is a wardrobe with pitiless glass,
Within it a rabbit lies trembling, alas!
My heart is a monstrance for profligate girls.
You laugh at my verses? You ignorant churls!
My heart is a stream that has only one wing:
I pity hyenas that drink from the thing!

Etc., etc.

But there you go, making me talk about poetry, and I digress from my subject. What was I saying? Oh yes, the soubrette who played her part to perfection.

It was the month of July. It was extremely hot, and my goodness! we certainly made ourselves comfortable.

Suddenly, the door to my study flies open with a bang. A big strapping fellow, solidly built, bursts in, cursing enough to bring the house down. It was Mademoiselle X...'s coachman, who had just had a clever idea.

Me, I lost my head, and, not feeling particularly safe, signed an IOU for 25,000 francs, on the pretext that I had raped his sister. That was rather outrageous, you must agree!

And that, dear sir, is the famous story of my blackmail, in all its simplicity. You can see that there's not much to it.

Please accept, etc.,

FRANCISQUE SARCEY

M. Sarcey's letter is too courteous for me to add a word. If I have caused the slightest pain to the gallant gentleman of the rue de Douai, you see me in despair.

At the last moment: An intimate friend of M. Sarcey's, to whom I showed this letter, has affirmed that it is not in the eminent critic's handwriting. According to him, I'm the victim of a prankster. I am furious!

CHEZ EDISON

By a fortunate coincidence, I happened to run into my excellent friend Octave Uzanne on the very day that he went to see Edison.

Clearly moved by the experience, Uzanne described the famous *kinetograph*, which we read about in *Figaro* on May 8.

It seemed to me that the *kinetograph* was not a dazzlingly original invention, and that it bore a striking resemblance to a toy called the *zoetrope*, which can be obtained for 25 or 30 francs in many French shops.

Recording movement with a series of snapshots hardly seems the height of genius. Last year, at the Photography Exposition at the Champ de Mars, we had the opportunity to contemplate several projections of this kind: horses jumping hurdles, birds flying, etc. Some movements lasted almost a minute, since there were 60 photos per second.

It was marvelous, but there you have it: it wasn't called a *kinetograph*, it didn't come from America, via Uzanne, and Edison had nothing to do with it.

The day after I saw the correspondent for *Le Figaro*, I rang at the gate of Orange Park. A few minutes later, I was in the presence of the brilliant Edison.

The amiable American showed me his little device, and I could watch successive images replacing one another, giving the illusion either of little boys playing leapfrog, or little girls jumping rope, or perhaps a circus rider jumping through a hoop.

I was not mistaken: I had already seen it somewhere.

Edison was eager to lead me through his workshop, and to show me the inventions that he was currently confecting.

One of them, which I think is bound to be a success, is something he calls an *Oil Lamp*.

Edison had the ingenious idea of using the combustible and illuminative properties of various kinds of fatty substances. For his *Oil Lamp*, he uses rapeseed oil.

Thanks to an ingenious design, whose principal elements are a *wick* (a sort of cotton stub) and a *spring*, the oil rises, by capillary action, into the *wick*. When the latter is sufficiently impregnated, you light it with a *match*, and as long as there is *oil* in the *wick*, you can enjoy a source of illumination that is adequate for most family activities, and far less harsh than electric light.

This new discovery is not yet fully perfected. Edison hopes to have it ready in two or three years, and to produce several hundred *Oil Lamps* a day for sale in both the new and old world.

Unfortunately, I have no room to describe all of the wonders at Orange Park. However, I cannot fail to mention one little device, very simple, but useful in many ways.

The instrument is composed of two serrated metal pieces joined at one end. And that's it. As its name, *nutcracker*, indicates, it removes shells from nuts.

But this is an instrument that Edison will never invent, because it's already a French product, known generally as... a shell game.

Citizens of France, my brothers, we have all been duped!

TOTO IN LUXEMBOURG

Toto, a young gentleman of five and a half years, spent his hours of leisure, that is, his mornings and afternoons, in the Luxembourg Garden. There, by his pleasant and ingratiating manners, he made many connections in the world of schoolboys and collegians. His nurse left him to his own devices, and while she gossiped with her compatriots, Toto circulated among different groups, calling everyone by name, and solemnly distributing handshakes all around.

Unfortunately, this fine existence has come to an end. One day, Toto went to Luxembourg with his mama, and the latter was able to verify that the young man's education had made rapid progress in a regrettable direction.

"Say, mama!" said Toto.

"What, Toto?"

"Y'see that little blonde over there, with all those curls on her forehead?"

"What about her?"

"Y'know what she's called?"

"No, Toto."

"Well, me, I know... She's called Alida Golden-Calf."

"Alida...?"

"Golden-Calf... Y'know, like the golden calf that Moses knocked over, in the Bible story, when the Jews got all mad... Y'know?"

"And how do you know the name of that woman?"

"That woman?... First of all, she's not a woman."

"That young lady, then?"

"No young lady, neither... She's a hooker."

"A hooker!!!???"

"Yeah, a hooker... You, you only know about fishermen usin' hooks. Well, in Paris, there are hookers too, only they're not the same hookers."

"And in Paris, what hookers are there?"

"What, at your age, you don't know what hookers are?"

"Toto, be polite. You don't talk that way to your mother."

"But mama, I'm polite, I'm just surprised, f' Christ's sake."

"For Christ's sake!... What strange expressions you've started using! You will do me the pleasure of refraining from such vulgar language."

"Vulgar language!... Aw, heck! It's always vulgar language with you. I won't say nothin', that's all!"

Toto sulks for a minute, then suddenly resumes:

"By the way, I never told you what hookers are in Paris."

"What are they?"

"Well, they're ladies who are like maids in the cafes, only, y'know, nice maids, with their hair all combed, an' with chic dresses and little white aprons, an' then little bags hangin' on their belts."

"Ah!"

"And some of 'em are really nice."

"Oh, bah!"

"But they really are... If you like, we can go by the rue de Vaugirard. I know a cafe where they're always in the doorway. I can show you. I know one real well, she's called Titine."

And Toto's mama cries out in horror:

"What, you know one of those creatures?"

Toto seems amazed at the maternal indignation.

"Why do you call 'em creatures? They're not nasty at all, y'know."

"I absolutely forbid you, Toto, do you hear me, to frequent that society!"

"Okay, okay... Keep your shirt on, ma. I won't frequent that society, like you say."

"And if you don't show better manners, I'll have your father punish you."

"Oh la la! As if pop, when he was a student, didn' go see hookers! And me, when I'm a student, like I won't be bothered with that!"

The mother is bewildered by such precocious perversity. Suddenly a group of English tourists appears, on their way to the museum.

Toto makes a megaphone with his hands, and calls in his most strident tones:

"Hey, you limeys!... Hey, you limeys!"

The *limeys*, thus summoned, turn around, and, ignoring their microscopic blasphemer, continue their halting and triumphal march to the museum.

The mother has turned red with shame and embarrassment. Toto notices, and smiles condescendingly:

"Didn' expect that, huh?... Well, what would you have said the other day!... Imagine there's a whole car of English people stoppin' at the Pantheon... So, there was a guy there who was tellin' 'em, loudly in English, all about the Pantheon... An' there's this wino, who shows up and starts yellin' at 'em, like I just did: 'Hey, you limeys!.. Hey, you limeys!...' The limeys got really mad... So, the drunk went off, doin' this at 'em... An' he says, 'If you see the Prince of Wales, tell him to bugger off!'"

And Toto reenacts the scene perfectly.

He yells the last words with great gusto, emphasizing them with a familiar gesture, known in some circles as *flipping the bird*.

Toto's mother is beside herself. Feverishly, she seizes her son by the wrist, and flees, mortified.

And that is why the park of the Médicis is now forbidden to Toto, a young gentleman of five and a half years.

LOVE WORKS A MIRACLE

At dessert, someone mentioned the miracles accomplished by love. A flame of remembrance flickered in my eyes, and this is the story that I told:

I had arrived that morning in Liverpool, and had to leave the next day for Quebec, on a steamboat in the Green Moon Line.

What business did I have in Quebec? I wonder what possible interest that could be to you. Nevertheless, since I have nothing to hide in my past life, I'll tell you that I was to represent, in Quebec, one of the finest suppliers of Jerusalem artichokes in Pont-Audemer.

All day, I loafed in Liverpool. Charming, to loaf in Liverpool!

As the clock struck five, I found myself on a quay, near a pontoon where a little steamboat that carried passengers across, to the left bank of the Mersey, was just docking.

A young woman arrived who was more beautiful than the dawn, far more beautiful than the dawn! Which, in fact, is not difficult, because, as far as I'm concerned (I don't know if you're like me), I never found the dawn that wonderful.

And how delicate she was!

She seemed confected from the pulp of some unknown pink dream.

Impossible to believe, for a moment, that her smallest molecule belonged to this earthly domain.

My God! My God! I loved her at once!

And her eyes! And her hair!

Her hair, above all! Hair like a blonde chimera with, in the sunlight, reflections of bright gold.

Oh! Her hair!

A mad surge of breathless tenderness hurled me into the depths, far into the depths. And I yearned to wrap myself in her hair, and to die there, peacefully.

People who know me, even casually, will not be surprised that, the next day, I missed the departure of my steamer.

Her name was Betsy Campbell, and we soon became the best friends in the world.

I met her father, her mother, her brothers, her sisters, and, in general, everything that constitutes a family in the northwest of England.

Then, time not ceasing to be money, and business obstinately remaining business, I was obliged to embark for the inopportune Canada.

To describe Betsy Campbell's tears would be a task beyond my powers.

Never, even in my worst debauches (during my seven months in Quebec, I was never sober), did I forget my pretty one's hair.

And then, faced with the Canadians' stupid prejudice against Jerusalem artichokes, I decided to return to Europe.

A telegram had preceded me; the entire Campbell family awaited me on the dock.

Oh, Betsy! Terrible Betsy!

At the sight of her, my face turned as pale as a serpent's.

She had decided, that little vixen, to cut her hair, her hair, do you hear me, her hair!

Now, she looked like a pretty, but impudent, little boy.

"Betsy," I told her after dinner, "you are no longer the Betsy of my dreams, with your short hair."

Great tears filled her big blue eyes, and I retired to the Northwestern Hotel (across from the equestrian statue of Her Majesty Victoria).

The next day, when I went to take my leave of those worthy Campbells, a harsh cry of surprise escaped my throat.

Betsy, Betsy, with her abundant, golden hair, even longer than before!

By the power of love, during the night, Betsy had managed to regrow her hair.

Dear, dear, dear little Betsy.

THE WIDOW MAKER

Who is there that never knew, ten years ago in Montmartre, Jules Dupaf? Who? Nobody.

He was a painter, not a very good one, admittedly, but he replaced talent with truly astonishing ingenuity; the boy had a genius for gimmicks.

Dupaf came up with gimmicks for everything in life, even for those things that seemed to demand the most simplicity.

He enjoyed relative prosperity, which made him sought after by every Bohemian on the Butte.

"Painting," he explained to me one day, "is not difficult in itself. The hardest thing is to sell it. Well, I found a gimmick that abolishes commissions, while infallibly increasing sales."

And it was true!

Quite skillful at *capturing a likeness*, Dupaf installed himself in a cafe frequented by rich merchants, got their names and addresses from the waiters, and furtively sketched two or three rapid pastels of those that seemed like *good subjects*. The next day, he executed portraits in oil of those stalwart fellows.

He no longer had a problem placing the merchandise; it was elementary:

"Good morning, M. Duconnel. I hope I am not being indiscreet, but finding myself beside you in the Cafe du Poste the other day, I was struck by the truly original character of your physiognomy. As soon as I returned home, I could think of nothing else but capturing your features on canvas. This is what I did. It's quite a resemblance, I think."

I will refrain from describing Duconnel's egotistical joy at the thought that his face could inspire artists. He called in his wife and kids, who were ecstatic!

"Oh, it's really you, daddy!"

And M. Duconnel is out five louis, sometimes ten.

To make the sale even more certain, Dupaf thought of another gimmick, which I find ingenious.

He adorned the buttonholes of his improvised subjects with a bit of red ribbon.

"But," they objected, "I haven't been decorated."

"What?" said Dupaf, apparently dumbfounded. "You haven't been decorated? That's hard to believe!"

And it was in the bag.

One fine day, Dupaf disappeared from Montmartre.

I assumed that he had gone abroad to exploit some international gimmick of his invention.

Approximately two years after his departure, I found myself in Le Havre; as a transatlantic arrived, I heard myself hailed vigorously by one of the passengers.

It was Dupaf! A sumptuously dressed Dupaf, with, on his burgeoning belly, a gold chain, fit for a hundred ton anchor, and luggage, luggage, luggage! (Not on his belly, the luggage!)

We had lunch together, and, at dessert, Dupaf told me the true story of his odyssey.

"I had had enough of painting. Always working the same scam on the same idiots is no fun after a while. Commerce and industry, old man, that's the way to go!

"I had at the time, if you remember, a mistress named Ninie, the widow Mme. Picquot. For my own amusement, I called her Veuve Clicquot. It infuriated her, I never knew why, but I found it enormously entertaining.

"From a joke to a profitable business is but a single step... And I took it!

"One morning, I took Ninie to a notary and founded the company Veuve Picquot, with me as associate, for the sale of champagne.

"Veuve Picquot... Veuve Clicquot. The Americans, who are a young people, I told myself, would never notice the difference. And so I left for America with I don't know how many thousands of bottles.

"Alas! The American people, despite their relative youth, doggedly rejected my poor Veuve Picquot. I was forced to liquidate my stock at prices that were not even derisory.

"Just between us, to be totally honest, the Veuve Picquot label concealed a product that was insanely undrinkable.

"You know me well enough to know that I was not discouraged by this misadventure.

"Ah! You don't want Veuve Picquot, I said to myself. Very well, I'll bring you Veuve Clicquot!

"And I mounted a campaign to discover a Widow Clicquot.

"No Widow Clicquot.

"Ah! There's no Widow Clicquot? Well then! We'll have to make one!

"I discovered a Clicquot family in Corrèze. I chose the most decrepit member of the family, and took him to Paris. Nothing was left but to find the future widow. Do you know MacLarinett?"

"My word, no. Who is he?"

"MacLarinett is a former Scottish admiral who has had his difficulties. I was his aide-de-camp during the Commune."

"And... what did he do during the Commune?"

"It was he who commanded the laundry boat at Pont-Marie."

"Oh, pshaw!"

"Yes... but let's return to our story. MacLarinett has seven daughters, all holy terrors. Imagine black panthers from Java, but blond, with eyebrows, darker than their hair, that meet at the top of the nose. All of them pretty, with, at times, a strange gleam in their eyes that is not at all reassuring.

"I married my Clicquot to one of the little MacLarinetts. Three months later, there was no more Clicquot than you have in your hand. But I had my Veuve Clicquot!

"Another trip to America. This time I came back with twenty thousand dollars. I sold my trademark to some Russians, who swindled me, and I lost a lot of money on the stock market.

"To get back into business, I needed a second Veuve Clicquot. I brought back from Corrèze another Clicquot, whom I married to the second of the little MacLarinetts. Two and a half months after the wedding, we gave Clicquot II a modest but respectable funeral. What a family, those MacLarinetts!

"And then, the matrimonial mania overtook me. I married five little MacLarinetts to five Clicquots, who were *polished off* in less time than it takes to write it. Only one sister is left, the youngest and prettiest of them all... If your heart speaks..."

"No, thank you."

And so spoke Dupaf, as calmly as if he were telling me about the founding of Phocaea by Greek colonists.

I never dreamed for a moment of objecting to his methods: they were scurrilous, but so ingenious! Dupaf and I parted that very evening. He went back to Paris, and I spent the summer down there.

In October, when I returned to Paris, one of the first friends that I met was precisely Jules Dupaf. But what a change!

Thin, sagging, his eyes sunken, his steps halting: was this really Dupaf, or his shadow?

I hesitated at our meeting; he came up to me, and shook my hand:

"How are you?... You know, you should come see us. I'm married now."

"Oh, bah!"

"It's true. I married the last of the little MacLarinetts." He added with a sadly brave smile, "It's a good thing my name isn't Clicquot."

And it was only then that I understood the verse of Ecclesiastes:

Those who live by the sword die by the sword.

Poor Dupaf!

We buried him November 2.

AN EXCELLENT OPPORTUNITY

In the aftermath of several financial catastrophes, and particularly since the unfortunate case of Panama, which received some publicity, the small investors of France have become wary.

The possibility of better returns draws dubious smiles, and if the late Andover Fyst himself, the well-known financier, returned to earth, spiders would probably have the leisure to spin webs over his tellers' windows.

This mistrust is somewhat exaggerated, for after all, as my concierge says, not everybody is a crook, thank God! And the failure of one plan is no reason to refuse to take advantage of a good opportunity.

Thus, I, I who now speak to you, know a truly secure investment, a real goldmine, in other words.

And please, don't interrupt me to accuse me of being part of the syndicate. Yes, I'm in the syndicate, and I'm proud of it; I'm in the syndicate like you, like them, like everyone. What would we do between meals if we weren't in a syndicate?

So, here is the business in question.

Brussels, as you are certainly not unaware, models herself on Paris, her big sister. She is her example in all of her intimate essence.

The two principal stations in Brussels are the Southern Station and the Northern Station. It's a curious thing, but the Southern Station in Brussels connects with the Northern Station in Paris. Logic would seem to dictate that the Belgian Northern Station would connect with our Paris-Lyon-Marseilles. But not at all, that line goes to Anvers and Ostende.

This is a little organizational error that I now bring to the attention of the Administrators of the Belgian railway.

Luxembourg Station in Brussels matches the one now being constructed in Paris, in Luxembourg Garden, to replace the old Sceaux station.

These three enterprises are all excellent opportunities, the Belgians being travelers by nature.

They don't travel as far as we do in France, because of the smaller borders of Belgium, but they go more often, and at the drop of a hat.

Given this state of affairs, we can easily deduce that if we built five new stations in Brussels: Saint-Lazare, Eastern, d'Orléans, Montparnasse, and Vincennes, those enterprises would not fail to obtain the success of their elders.

Have we not noticed, in Paris, that the more we multiply our trains, buses, streetcars, etc., the more crowded they are?

Therefore, as I stated above, the *Society for New Stations in Brussels* is a secure investment, really top of the line.

Steps are underway to get it registered officially with the Paris Bourse.

LOUDER AND LOUDER

This morning, I met a man, still young, who pays me 600 francs a year just to keep his name out of the papers, but whom we will nevertheless designate by the sobriquet of *Captain Cap*.

Captain Cap is a curious soul, who seems to incarnate a penchant for meteorology, a thorough knowledge of marine matters, and an aptitude for the racetrack (not to mention a keen appetite for cosmopolitan drinks).

Having traveled widely, Captain Cap has retained a great deal, from insights into Australian esthetics to the jig tunes of San Francisco.

Captain Cap is what is known as *somebody*.

Since I met him, I cannot recall spending five minutes in his company without some new little surprise, sometimes trivial, but always something (and without the slightest change in his expression, besides).

So, this morning, we found ourselves on the terrace of a cafe on the Champs-Elysées (we often go to cafes, Captain Cap and I).

No waiter to serve us.

Cap pulls a ten centime piece from his pocket, and strikes the marble table with some violence.

The summons is in vain.

Calmly, Cap replaces the humble copper knocker with a five franc coin. And he raps, and he raps, and he raps.

The unsettling torpor of the cafe does not awaken by one iota.

Then, our bold Captain Cap, who wants the last word—as well as a drink, finally!—extracts from his billfold a thousand franc note, with which he furiously hammers the table.

It is only at this notification that the waiter decides to place himself at our service.

A VERY MODERN LITTLE WIFE

Once upon a time there was a little wife who was awfully nice, and who had forgotten to be stupid, you can bet on that.

Her husband, though, was as ugly as sin, and as stupid as a pig.

The sentiments that the little wife harbored for her husband would not have sufficed (as far as temperature is concerned) to melt two dabs of butter, whereas he would have thrown himself into fire or water for his little wife, at one sign from her.

Situations like this are, by the way, frequently encountered in many contemporary households.

The nice little wife and the ugly husband wallowed in the most regrettable indigence. Gold did not overflow their strongbox; in fact, they didn't even have a strongbox.

The man, frankly, would not have minded being poor — he was happy with four sous of sausage and an alpaca jacket — but, for the sake of his pretty little wife, he suffered from his poverty, and the neighbors often heard him repeating:

"Oh my God, it's annoying to be so destitute!"

His only income was from his position as an accountant, in a firm that had just been established to import phylloxera into Northern Spain (and which has since liquidated).

If his salary came to 1,800 or 2,000, that was the end of the rainbow.

I've never met you, but I'd like to see your expression if you made 2,000 francs a year, especially if you found yourself married to a little wife who preferred twill to moleskin.

Fortunately, he was very stupid — as I said earlier — and cut his charming companion's blather short.

"How much," she said, "do I think I paid for these dozen blouses?"

"Shoot," responded our imbecile, scratching his head, "I don't know."

"Not as much as that, dear! It's unbelievable. Forty-eight sous. You can't say that I'm ruining you, eh?"

"Forty-eight sous?" he repeated, stunned.

"Yes, my friend, forty-eight sous! They were on sale."

To be honest, the little wife was stretching the truth, with her forty-eight sous. The blouses in question had not cost her forty-eight sous, not even forty sous, not even twenty sous, not even ten sous.

Not even two sous, not even one sou!

They had cost her... let's say, a smile (because of the young ladies who are listening).

Despite frequent repetition of these smiles in town, the couple's hardship grew to cruel proportions.

Then, one day, when dinner had been more meager than usual (which is not saying much), the little wife went into her husband's room, just as he was getting into bed, and here is the conversation that took place between them:

(Imagine that the pretty little wife offered these words in the voice of a fairy, whereas the husband's timbre recalled a slide trombone which had remained in the Meuse since the deplorable incidents of 1870).

"Say, my dear," she said, running her exquisite hands through the man's hideous hair.

"Darling?"

"Do you know what I just read in the bathroom, in an old newspaper?"[1]

"What, my beautiful darling?"

"A story about a man in Versailles, who took out life insurance, and then collected on it when he showed them a corpse that he passed off as his own."

"What of it?"

"Well, the man collected on his insurance."

"Yes, but wasn't he caught?"

"He was caught, because he was a fool. But I've come up with a brilliant plan to avoid getting caught."

"!!!???"

.....

At this point, they blew out the candle, and I heard nothing more.

The little wife explained her plan in a whisper, and the man had no objections.

Soon, there was the sound of kisses (let's say *kisses*, because of the young ladies who are still listening).

.....

A few weeks after the events that I have just related, a man was found murdered in a railroad car, on the little local line that goes from Dunkirk to Biarritz.

The papers found on him established his identity.

The pretty little wife fingered, with convulsive sobs, the 200,000 francs of insurance.

She wore that day a truly exquisite black outfit, fragrant with Cosmydor.

That evening, she tossed into the mail (foreign) the following note:

"My dear late husband,

"You know how frightened I have always been of ghosts.

"You were always good to me when you were alive: I hope that you will not bother me after your death.

"Besides, the climate in Paris, so beneficial to my health, is disastrous for any deceased with your temperament.

"She who will never forget you,

HÉLÈNE"

.....

Would you sacrifice yourself like that for the ladies?

---

1. I apologize to my female readers for the unpoetical vulgarity of this detail, but when one writes for posterity, as I do, one renounces forever the right to embroider or to change the facts. See in me nothing but a pale slave of the truth (*lividus servus veritatis*).

"Like the Others" (*Comme les autres*): *Le Journal*, May 25, 1893.

Madeleine-Bastille is a bus line in Paris, and *j'en passe et des meilleurs* means "I have a million of them."

Double Over (*À se tordre*) was Allais's first collection, published by Ollendorff in 1891.

"The Social Question" (*La question sociale*): *Le Journal*, February 3, 1893.

Marie François Sadi Carnot had indeed been a distinguished student at the École Polytechnique. He served as President of France from 1887 until his assassination in 1894. His grandfather, Lazare Nicolas Marguerite, Comte Carnot, was a minister of war during the Revolution, and became known as "the organizer of the victory." I suspect that the scene at the Moulin Rouge was fictional.

As Allais mentions, on December 8, 1892 his column was devoted to another meeting with Carnot: Allais discussed his plans to reform the military by abolishing the artillery (too noisy) and both infantry and cavalry (unpleasant for the soldiers).

Joseph-Lambert Dupuis, known professionally as José Dupuis, was a Belgian tenor and actor; he was particularly associated with Offenbach.

"Tripoli" (*Tripoli*): *Le Journal*, December 16, 1892.

René Georges Hermann-Paul was a satirical painter and illustrator.

La pouille means "bad luck."

La République Française was a daily paper, founded in 1871 by Léon Gambetta. It was fairly left wing, although not radical.

The Military Governor of Paris commands the garrison, and organizes military parades and other ceremonies.

Val-de-Grâce is a military hospital in Paris.

"Business Cafe" (*Café d'affaires*): *Le Journal*, October 13, 1892. Originally entitled *Une excellente affaire* ("An Excellent Opportunity"), like the other story below.

Léon Gandillot was a popular playwright, and, not incidentally, a regular at the Chat Noir. Allais profiled him, inimitably, later in this collection.

A "bitter mint" (*amer-menthe*), sometimes called a *Picon-menthe,* was an apéritif made by Picon.

According to an article in the *Thames Star*, January 20, 1897, there was a rumor afloat that Edison and Tesla were developing a chrysoscope. I suspect Allais would have been pleased.

"Too Many Kangaroos" (*Trop de kanguroos*): *Le Journal*, February 25, 1893.

The Jardin d'acclimatation was founded by the zoologist Isidore Geoffroy Saint-Hilaire in 1860, and later directed by his son Albert.

Jean Sarrazin was both poet and olive merchant; he used to walk through the Chat Noir with a book of his poems in one hand and a basket of olives in the other.

Salerno is the site of Europe's oldest medical school.

"A Pleasant Memory" (*Doux Souvenir*): *Le Journal*, February 21, 1893. Originally entitled *Grands magasins. — Immense caravansérails. — Vastes halls. — L'Almée de Montmartre. — Une sale blague. — Excellente leçon* ("Great department stores. — Immense caravansaries. — Vast halls. — The almah of Montmartre. — A dirty trick.—Excellent lesson.")

The Grands Magasins du Louvre, one of France's largest department stores from 1855 to 1974, is not to be confused with the museum of the same name.

"Fire" (*Feu*): *Le Journal*, January 14, 1893.

Désiré-Magloire Bourneville was a neurologist, active in health care reform; André-Justin Martin was, among other things, the Inspector General of Sanitization and Salubrity in the Home; Henry Claude Robert Napias was the Director of Public Assistance.

"It Was Snowing...! Or the Ostination [sic] of a Cyclist" (*Il neigeait...! ou l'ostination (sic) d'un cycliste*): *Le Journal*, January 28, 1893.

Ostination is the Canadian form of *obstination*; Allais, a staunch Canadaphile, may have used it to evoke those snowy regions.

Caran d'Ache (Emmanuel Poirier) was a cartoonist, with a penchant for pantomime strips. Like Allais, he frequented the Chat Noir, where he designed many of the shadow puppet plays.

"Bleak plain" is indeed a familiar quote from Hugo. It comes from the second part of his poem *l'Expiation*: *Waterloo! Waterloo! Waterloo! Morne plaine!*

"On the Disadvantages of Excessive Baudelaireism" (*Inconvénients du baudelairisme outrancé*): Previously unpublished.

The quatrain that the young pharmacist recites is the fifth stanza of *Chanson d'après-midi* ("Afternoon Song") from *Les fleurs du mal*:

*Ah! les philtres les plus forts
Ne valent pas ta paresse,*

Et tu connais la caresse
Qui fait revivre les morts!

He does, however, quote it incorrectly, substituting *revenir* for *revivre*.

Baudelaire's mother lived in Honfleur, and the poet visited her when Allais was a boy. Allais's mother recalled that Baudelaire stopped into the family pharmacy at times, to argue with her husband and to try to buy opium. Allais eventually bought her house, known as the Maison Baudelaire.

"The Baby Bullet" (*L'enfant de la balle*): *Le Journal*, March 14, 1893.

As Allais states, this story was published in the *American Medical Weekly*, in 1874. Its author, Dr. Legrand G. Capers, later admitted that it was a joke.

The Minié rifle was invented by Claude-Étienne Minié and Henri-Gustave Delvigne in 1849. Its large lead bullets caused severe wounds, and often broke bones.

"The Awakening of 22" (*Le réveil de 22*): *Le Journal*, March 16, 1893.

"A Few Numbers" (*Quelques chiffres*): *Le Journal*, February 28, 1893. Originally entitled *La victoire de Terront. — Juste réclamation de M. Porel. — Un peu de calcul. — Un voeu bien légitime. — Inertie des Ponts-et-Chaussées.* ("Terront's victory. — M. Porel's just complaint. — A bit of arithmetic. — A quite legitimate wish. — Inertia from the General Council of Roads and Bridges.")

Charles Terront is considered the first star of French cycling;

Jean-Marie Corre was another champion cyclist, who later went into manufacturing both bicycles and automobiles. Their 1000 kilometer race in 1893 was followed by 50,000 fans.

Paul Porel was an actor and director, who briefly ran the Eden-Théâtre in Paris. His real name was Parfouru, allowing Allais to make a pun on *parcouru* (traveled through). I've done what I could with that.

"French Rabbits and Belgian Frogs" (*Lapins des France et grenouilles belges*): *Le Journal*, March 23, 1893.

Auguste Chauveau was President of the Académie des Sciences de Paris, and a disciple of Claude Bernard, a pioneer of experimental medicine. Chauveau was often attacked by anti-vivisectionists for his experiments with animals. Hédou was actually Édouard Hédon, an endicronologist; his name was misspelled in the report that Allais cites, so I shall misspell it here as well.

Unfortunately, Leopold II is not remembered for his kindness to frogs, but for his ruthless exploitation of the Congo and his atrocities against the Congolese.

"A Gloomy Poem" (*Poème morne*): *Le Chat Noir*, February 2, 1889.

Maurice Maeterlinck was, of course, one of the leading lights of Symbolism, and Belgian. When originally published in *Le Chat Noir*, it bore the subtitle "Translated from the Swiss," and the dedication "To make Auriol cry" (that being George Auriol, poet, designer, and Chat Noir regular).

Éloa is a long and very Romantic poem by Alfred de Vigny, from 1823.

"Excess in Anything Is a Fault" (*L'excès en tout est un défaut*): *Le Journal*, April 17, 1893.

For an "Exposition on Colonial Ethnography" in 1893, 150 Dahomeyans took up residence in the Champ-de-Mars, a large park in Paris.

"A True Pearl" (*Une Vraie Perle*): *Le Chat Noir*, December 5, 1891.

Our protagonist's name is a pun on Guy de Maupassant; a *noeud coulant* is a hangman's noose. Hortense may have been named after de Maupassant's story *La Reine Hortense*.

Melinite, an explosive made from cotton and picric acid, was developed by the chemist Eugène Turpin. It was also, probably not incidentally, the nickname for the dancer Jane Avril.

I haven't been able to trace Gabriell Bonnett, or any possible misspellings, but it's possible that he did work for the Oxnard Beet Sugar Company, which did do business in Grand Island, Nebraska.

Pertuis-Sec (dry inlet) is a real place, in Southern France; Allais, however, may have chosen it as descriptive of the Marquise.

Verlaine's poem is *Colloque sentimental*, from his second collection, *Fêtes galantes*, in 1869. As Allais indicates, it describes two ghosts. My version is no more than a metrical paraphrase; the original is:

Dans le grand parc solitaire et glacé,
Deux formes ont tout à l'heure passé.

"Science Aided by Political Ambition Works Miracles" (*La science, aidée par l'ambition politique, produit des miracles*): *Le Journal*, April 20, 1893.

Did a Dr. Lehuppé really run in the municipal elections? If so, his name was a liability: *huppé* means posh, snooty.

"Full" (*Complet*): *Le Chat Noir*, February 26, 1887.

Antoine Plège founded the traveling circus that bore his name in 1856; for many years it was one of France's most popular. Although Allais never worked for it, he did play drums for the shadow plays at the Chat Noir.

Leo von Caprivi was then Chancellor of Germany.

"A Hallucination" (*Une hallucination*): *Le Chat Noir*, April 28, 1888; *Le Journal*, April 5, 1893. The earlier version was entitled *Notes*.

I haven't traced Baïssass, but he may very well have worked for the *Journal*.

The gingerbread fair was a large carnival, including rides, museums of curiosities, and booths selling candy, pottery, and, of course, gingerbread. Allais's two "excellent comrades" were real people: Henri d'Eugène Philippe Louis d'Orléans, duc d'Aumale, son of King Louis-Philippe, was then 71; Charles Antoine Gidel, director of Condorcet and author of several scholarly works on French and Greek literature, was then 66.

In the earlier version, Allais's companions were Jules Jouy and George Auriol: "the witty singer, the charming cartoonist, and me."

"A New Kind of Illumination" (*Un nouvel éclairage*): *Le Chat Noir*, November 5, 1887; *Le Journal*, June 19, 1893.

A *foucade* is, appropriately, a caprice.

There is no such place as Taupin; however *mine de houille à Taupin* recalls the old expression *sec comme les couilles à Taupin* (as dry as Taupin's balls). The origin of the phrase, and the identity of the unfortunate Taupin, are unknown.

Cornuel is a fairly common name; I don't know who is meant here. In the earlier version, he was *le capitaine de frégate Lépluché.*

"Cruel Enigma" (*Cruelle énigme*): *Le Chat Noir*, May 9, 1891.

Raoul Ponchon had a long career as a poet and journalist. He was friends with Rimbaud and Verlaine, and is particularly remembered for his many verses in praise of absinthe.

Flanchard means "cowardly."

I have been forced into a neologism, "temperamentuous," to properly render Allais's *tempéramenteuse*, one of many coinages by the eccentric writer Restif de la Bretonne. Allais may have chosen it because it contains the word *menteuse*, "liar," so I'll just mention that.

Edouard Philippe was a composer; I suppose he was also short. Jean Joseph Pierre Pascalis was a lawyer, lynched by a mob during the Revolution; he was famously tall and commanding.

"An Important Reform in the Western Railway Company" (*Une importante réforme à la compagnie de l'ouest*): *Le Journal*, February 6, 1893. Originally entitled *Le crime de la rue Saint-Lazare.—Brutale mesure.—L'échelle des amours.—Une solution.—Bonne renommé de M. Dreux.* ("The crime on rue Saint-Lazare.—Brutal step.—The love ledger.—A solution.—M. Dreux's good reputation.")

Allais refers to a real crime. Louise Lamier was murdered on January 27, 1893, and her body was discovered by Perrin, an employee at the Saint-Lazare station.

I suppose Charles Raymond had something to do with the railway, but I couldn't trace him.

Allais's maritime suggestions for Perrin are inspired by the fact that the French word for "pimp" is "mackerel" (*maquereau*).

Perrin's co-worker, Achille Dreux, was also involved with Louise

Lamier, and was briefly held as a suspect.

"Like a Fish" (*Dalle en pente*): *Le Chat Noir*, October 8, 1887; *Gil Blas*, July 20, 1892. Originally entitled *A votre santé* ("To Your Health").

Jane A. is, of course, Jane Avril, dancer at the Moulin-Rouge, and romantically linked to Allais. She was, however, a redhead.

"The age of the captain" refers to a mock math problem, posed by Flaubert in a letter to his sister: "A ship leaves Boston with a cargo of wool, weighing 200 tons. It sails for Le Havre, the mainmast is broken, the cabin boy is on deck, there are twelve passengers, the wind is from the NEE, the clock reads 3:15 pm, and the month is May. How old is the captain?"

Léon Delarue was the stage manager at the Chat Noir.

Édouard Dujardin's play *Le Chevalier du passé* was performed at the Théâtre Moderne in 1892.

The young woman was originally Mlle. Marie Kr... (Krysinka); her bridegroom was Henry G... V... (Gauthier-Villars): pianist-poet and critic, respectively.

"The False Blasphemer" (*La Fausse Blasphématrice*): *Le Chat Noir*, December 4, 1886; *Le Journal*, March 21, 1893. The earlier version was entitled *Pluie* ("Rain").

Jean Gautherin's statue of Diderot was widely ridiculed; it showed him seated in a pretentious and histrionic pose. It was destroyed by the Nazis in 1941.

Il n'a pas d'parapluie ("He Has No Umbrella"), by Louis Gabillard and Félix Menier, was quite popular in the 1880s.

"Half and Half" (*Half and half*): *Le Journal*, April 10, 1893.

The Institut National des Jeunes Aveugles was founded in 1784, making it the first school for the blind; it does have a theater.

My couplet is only an evocation of Allais's superior original:

Soubeyran, marchand de vin, pale ale, porter,
Sous Berr, en marchant, devint pâle à le porter.
(Soubeyran, seller of wine, pale ale, porter,
Under Berr, while walking, becomes pale from carrying him.)

Jean-Marie Georges Girard, baron de Soubeyran, was a conservative politician; Georges Berr was an actor in the Comédie-Française.

In 1892, Allais confessed himself overtaken with a *maboulite holorimeuse* (holorimic obsession), and wrote many holorimic couplets. As he put it, "Like the pig, in which all is good, from the head to the tail, in my poem all is rhyme, from the first syllable to the last."

"Essay on a New Division of France" (*Essai sur une nouvelle division de la France*): *Gil Blas*, January 17, 1892; *Le Journal*, May 13, 1893. The title in *Gil Blas* was *Le Midi à quatorze heures* ("The Midi at fourteen o'clock"); and in *Le Journal*, *Division de la France sans la diviser* ("Division of France without dividing it").

Allais rewrote this for his final book, *Captain Cap* (1902), making it into a talk by the Captain. Captain Cap was a real person, Albert Caperon, and was featured in many of Allais's stories.

"Let us always think it, but never say it" was the slogan for the reannexation of Alsace and Lorraine.

"The Good-Natured Manager" (*Le patron bon au fond*): *Le Chat Noir*, August 2, 1890; *Le Journal*, February 18, 1893. The earlier version was entitled *Le patron narquois, mais bon au fond* ("The Sarcastic Manager Who Was Basically Good-Natured"); it was accompanied by an "English Novel" by George Auriol and an "Irish Novel" by Maurice O'Reilly.

Our two Highlanders are called *ma castrole* (my casserole) and *ma crinoline* (my crinoline).

Luigi Loir is invoked here simply because *loir* means "dormouse."

The legendary Taupin, he of the proverbially dry balls, reappears (see "A New Form of Illumination," above).

In the *Chat Noir* version, the two Scots are MacAlphonse and MacAskett.

"Reversibility (Reversibilité): *Le Journal*, October 18, 1892.

Unfortunately, the young duke's name sounds like *du conneau de la lunerie* (of the idiot of foolishness).

The "phony magus" is Josephin Péladan, who called himself the Sâr Péladan, and organized salons variously described as Rosicrucian, Wagnerian, and Chaldean. Allais refers to him here as the *faux mage de Livarot* (the phony magus of Livarot), a pun on *fromage de Livarot*, Livarot cheese being as proverbially stinky in French as Limburger is in English. Péladan was frequently ridiculed as unkempt; the poet Laurent Tailhade cited him as "renowned in literature for the strong odor of his feet."

Erik Satie was born, like Allais, in Honfleur, and played piano and harmonium at the Chat Noir and the Auberge du Clou. He wrote fanfares for Péladan's Rosicrucian events, and incidental music for Péladan's play *Le Fils des Étoiles* (*The Sun of the Stars*). Among his other compositions were the *Ogives* and *Gymnopédies*, here neologized into adjectives.

Eugène Auguste Albert Rochas d'Aiglun had a long career as military engineer, translator, and historian; in later life, he wrote many works on paranormal subjects.

"The Templars" (*Les templiers*): *Le Chat Noir*, August 13, 1887.

"To contemplate your azure, O Mediterranean" (*Contempler ton azur, ô Méditerranée*) is a line from Victor Hugo, from *Ruy Blas*.

It was, in fact, the Knights Hospitallers who built the Palace of the Grand Master on Rhodes.

"The Story of Little Stephen Girard" (*Histoire du petit Stephen Girard*): *Le Chat Noir*, September 27, 1890; *Le Journal*, March 6, 1893.

This story has a complicated history. First of all, Stephen Girard was a real man, a wealthy banker and philanthropist in Philadelphia. Second, the story is not by Mark Twain.

Twain scholar Barbara Schmidt has determined that it was actually written by John W. Beach, a Brooklyn humorist who contributed to the *New York Sun*. "Stephen Girard" appeared as part of a column called "John in Philadelphia," which first appeared in the paper on October 21, 1872. The part about Stephen Girard was reprinted in other newspapers, and frequently attributed to Twain. Twain himself never denied it, which only complicated matters.

Allais followed the original closely, although he did tone down some of the broader humor. Here it is, for comparison:

STORY OF POOR LITTLE STEPHEN GIRARD.

The man lives in Philadelphia who when young and poor entered a bank, and says he, "Please, sir, do you want a boy?" and the stately personage said, "No, little boy, I don't want a little boy." The little boy, whose heart was too full for utterance, chewing a piece of licorice stick he had bought with a cent stolen from his good but pious aunt, with sobs plainly audible, and with great globules of water rolling down his cheeks, glided silently down the marble steps of the bank. Bending his noble form, the bank man dodged behind a door, for he thought the little boy was going to shy a stone at him. But the boy picked up something, and stuck it in his poor but ragged jacket. Then spake the bank man, "Come here, little boy;" and the little boy did come here; and the bank man said, "Lo, what pickest thou up?" And he answered and replied, "A pin." And the bank man said, "How do you vote?— excuse me, do you go to Sunday school?" and he said he did. Then the bank man took down a pen made of pure gold and flowing with pure ink, and he wrote on a piece of paper, "St. Peter," and he asked the little boy what it stood for, and he said, "Salt Peter." Then the bank man said it meant "Saint Peter." The little boy said "Oh!" Then the bank man took the little boy to his bosom, and the little boy said "Oh" again, for he squeezed him. Then the bank man took the little boy into partnership, and gave him half the profits and all the capital, and he married the bank man's daughter, and now all he has is all his and is all his own, too.

STORY OF ANOTHER GOOD LITTLE BOY

My uncle told me this story, and I spent six weeks picking up pins in front of a bank. I expected the bank man would call me in and say, "Little boy, are you good?" and I was going to say, "Yes," and when he asked me what "St. John" stood for, I was going to say, "Salt John." But I guess the bank man wasn't anxious to have a partner, and I guess his daughter was a son, for one day says he to me, says he, "Little boy, what's that you're picking up?" Says I, awful meekly, "Pins." Says he, "Let's see 'em." And he took 'em, and I took off my cap all ready to go into the bank, and become a partner, and marry his daughter. But I didn't get an invitation. He said, "You little rascal, those pins belong to the bank, and if I catch you hanging around here any more I'll set the dog on you." Then I left, and the mean old cuss kept the pins. Such is life as I find it.

"Posthumous" (*Posthume*): *Le Chat Noir*, April 10, 1886.
The bal Tonnelier was held every Sunday in Montparnasse.
Moreau is glossy black, or a horse of that color, although Allais may also be invoking the painter Gustave Moreau.

"Léon Gandillot": *Le Journal*, April 23 and May 6, 1893. The second part was originally entitled *Une lettre de M. Sarcey. — Légitime rectification. — Un bon tour. — Quelques vers. — Canaillerie d'un cocher. — On se f... de moi.* ("A letter from M. Sarcey. — Legitimate correction. — A good trick. — A few verses. — A coachman's dishonesty. — I am mocked.")

Gandillot was a popular playwright; naturally, he looked nothing like Allais's description, and did none of the things attributed to him here. He did, however, write the two plays mentioned, *Le Sous-Préfet de Château-Buzard* and *Femmes Collantes*.

Rather than give the entire history of the 1848 Revolution and the Franco-Prussian War, I'll simply mention that Alexandre Auguste Ledru-Rollin was a champion of the proletariat, whose speeches helped foment the revolution, and that Louis-Antoine Garnier-Pagès and François Arago were active in the Second Republic that followed.

Lambessa, in Algeria, had a large prison for French political deportees.

Francisque Sarcey was one of the most influential theatrical critics in Paris. He preferred light, commercial fare, which made him a target for every Bohemian in the city. Allais vigorously ridiculed him in the pages of *Le Chat Noir*, depicting him as a lecherous, gluttonous, simple-minded clown, often in pieces under Sarcey's byline. To his credit, Sarcey took all of this in good humor.

Peau-de-Lapin (Rabbit Skin) was a regular at the Café de la Nouvelle-Athènes, a dealer, apparently, in paintings and antiques. I found a mention of him in *Paris-Palette*, by Charles Virmaitre (1888): "The dealer in paintings is Peau-de-Lapin, a surname, hirsute head, good-hearted, obliging, mocking."

"Chez Edison": *Le Journal*, May 9, 1893. Originally entitled *Visite chez Edison*.

Allais's close friend, the poet-humorist-inventor Charles Cros, invented a phonograph, the Paleophone, a few months before Edison. Having no money to build a prototype, he sealed the idea in an envelope and left it with the French Academy of Sciences. Allais always disliked Edison for patenting his device first.

Octave Uzanne was indeed a journalist for *Le Figaro*, as well as a publisher, writer, and noted bibliophile.

"Toto in Luxembourg" (*Toto en Luxembourg*): *Le Chat Noir*, August 28, 1886.

"Love Works a Miracle" (*Un miracle de l'amour*): *Le Journal*, March 27, 1893.

"The Widow Maker" (*Fabrique de veuves*): *Le Chat Noir*, June 25, 1887. Originally entitled *Les Petites Dardinska*, those being the precursors to the MacLarinetts.

Jules du paf probably means "the guy with the penis"; but *paf* can also mean "drunk."

The Butte is Montmartre.

Duconnel is apparently a *conneau* (idiot).

A *picot* is a tooth.

The Pont-Marie is one of the bridges across the Seine; in earlier times, laundry boats were common on the river.

The verse about the sword, as you Bible buffs know, is actually Matthew 26:52.

"An Excellent Opportunity" (*Une excellente affaire*): *Le Journal*, January 3, 1893. Originally entitled *La petite épargne a de la méfiance. — Une affaire d'or. — A l'instar. — La Société des nouvelles gares de Bruxelles. — N'hésitons pas à souscrire.* ("Small investors are wary. — A profitable business. — Follow the example. — The Society for New Stations in Brussels. — Let us not hesitate to subscribe.")

Andover Fyst is my anglicization of Laurent Bart; that is, *l'or en barre*, bar of gold, as in the expression *faire de l'or en barre*, to make a lot of money.

"Louder and Louder" (*De plus en plus fort*): Previously unpublished.

This is one of the first appearances of Captain Cap, whom we met above in connection with a new division of France. Cap was, in fact, not as widely traveled as Allais claims here; he was born in France, grew up in California and England, and inherited a fortune, much of which he squandered on cocktails.

"A Very Modern Little Wife" (*Une petite femme bien moderne*): *Le Chat Noir*, April 27, 1889; *Gil Blas*, June 10, 1892. The *Chat Noir* version was simply entitled *Une femme moderne* ("A Modern Wife").

Dunkirk and Biarritz are at the extreme north and south of France.

The deplorable incidents of 1870 at the Meuse are generally known as the Battle of Sedan. Historians are silent on the role played by trombones.

Cosmydor was a manufacturer of soaps and perfumes.

ABOUT THE AUTHOR

ALPHONSE ALLAIS (1854 – 1905) began his career in Paris during the Belle Epoque. He was particularly active at the legendary cabaret Le Chat Noir, where he wrote for and edited the weekly paper. He quickly became known for his deadpan wit and inexhaustible imagination. Among other things, he also exhibited some of the first monochromatic pictures (such as his all-white "First Communion of Chlorotic Girls in the Snow" in 1883) and composed the first silent piece of music: "Funeral March for the Obsequies of a Deaf Man" (1884).

Throughout most of his life, he contributed columns several times a week to *Le Journal* and *Le Sourire*. These pieces were collected into twelve volumes, which he called his "Anthumous Works," between 1892 and 1902. He also published a collection of his monochromes, *Album Primo-Avrilesque*, in 1897, and a novel, *L'Affaire Blaireau*, in 1899, as well as a few plays. His later years were troubled by debt, a bad marriage, and heavy drinking; he died at 59.

He was a crucial influence on Alfred Jarry, as well as on the Surrealists: Breton included him in his *Anthology of Black Humor*, and Duchamp was reading him on the day he died. Allais's fascination with wordplay, puns, and holorhymes led Oulipo to call him an "anticipatory plagiarist"; the Pataphysical College dubbed him their "Patacessor." His books have remained in print in France, and the Académie Alphonse Allais has awarded a literary prize in his honor since 1954.

ABOUT THE TRANSLATOR

DOUG SKINNER has contributed articles and cartoons to *Black Scat Review, Oulipo Pornobongo, The Fortean Times, Strange Attractor Journal, Fate, Weirdo, The Anomalist, Crimewave USA, Nickelodeon, Zuzu, Cabinet,* and other fine publications. His book of picture stories, *The Unknown Adjective and Other Stories,* was published by Black Scat Books in 2014.

His translations include *Three Dreams* (Giovanni Battista Nazari, Magnum Opus Hermetic Sourceworks, 2002), *Considerations on the Death and Burial of Tristan Tzara* (Isidore Isou, Black Scat, 2012), *How I Became an Idiot* (Alphonse Allais, Black Scat, 2013), *Captain Cap* (Alphonse Allais, Black Scat, 2013), *Merde à la Belle Époque* (various, Black Scat, 2013), and *Selected Plays* (Alphonse Allais, Black Scat, 2014).

He has written music for several dance companies, including ODC-San Francisco and Margaret Jenkins; his scores for actor/ clown Bill Irwin include *The Regard of Flight, The Courtroom, The Regard Evening,* and *The Harlequin Studies.*

He lives in Manhattan, venturing from his garret occasionally to teach music lessons and to perform his music in discerning clubs and cabarets.